K

By
Eve Langlais

Copyright and Disclaimer

Copyright © June 2014, Eve Langlais
Cover Art by Aubrey Rose © May 2014
Edited by Devin Govaere
Copy Edited by Amanda L. Pederick
Produced in Canada

Published by Eve Langlais
1606 Main Street, PO Box 151
Stittsville, Ontario, Canada, K2S1A3
http://www.EveLanglais.com

ISBN-13: 978-1499729207
ISBN-10: 1499729200

Kodiak's Claim is a work of fiction and the characters, events and dialogue found within the story are of the author's imagination and are not to be construed as real. Any resemblance to actual events or persons, either living or deceased, is completely coincidental.

No part of this book may be reproduced or shared in any form or by any means, electronic or mechanical, including but not limited to digital copying, file sharing, audio recording, email and printing without permission in writing from the author.

Chapter One

"Call me a fat and boring cow will he?" Tammy huffed as she tossed his favorite jersey on the layer of neatly stacked coals. "Cheat on me with my so-called friend." The jerk. On to the pile went his CD holder of Xbox games. "How dare he think he can treat me like dirt and laugh about it." Ha. *Let's see who laughs last.* She squirted lighter fluid onto the pyre she'd built on the grill.

"And they say breaking up is hard to do." She held a lit match that said otherwise. The flame danced and flickered as she dropped it, but the tiny stick remained afire and ignited her impromptu bonfire with a *whoosh*. Despite the fire's captivity within the barbecue, a frisson of fear still shot up her spine. But she didn't run for the hose or an extinguisher. She faced her fear, just like her shrink taught her to.

As the pile of stuff crackled and burned, she heard the slam of the screen door and the stomp of feet as he trampled down the back porch steps. "What the hell are you doing, you crazy bitch?"

Ooh a new name. At least this one she deserved. Turning to face him, the heat of her barbecue warming her plump backside, Tammy pasted a cold smirk on her face. "I'd say what I was doing is obvious. I'm cleansing myself of you."

"With my shit!" he yelled, gesturing to the burning pyre.

She shrugged. "Yeah, well, since you weren't around when I got the text, I found another way to vent." A break-up text, which he'd sent after storming out after their fight a few hours ago when she'd confronted him about his dalliance with her friend. To think he'd had the nerve to defend himself, citing her lack of drive when it came to losing weight as to why he'd wandered and stuck his penis in someone else.

I never promised to change myself for him. I like myself just fine as I am. And 'as I am' consisted of a few extra pounds, a very voluptuous frame, and a healthy appetite. Would she like to perhaps sport a skinnier frame? Sure. However, she wasn't about to give up everything she loved—French fries, pizza, chips and ooh, chocolate ice cream—and start a rigorous exercise regime just to please a man. *Love me as I am,* or at least pretend to.

He waved his hands around wildly. "I'm calling the cops. You don't have the right to do this."

"Do what? Barbecue my dinner?" She pointed to the steak sitting on a plate beside the barbecue, thick, red, and sprinkled with a touch of garlic, pepper, and sea salt. Inside her townhouse, rice bubbled in a pot and a salad smothered in a garlic Caesar dressing awaited. Nothing like charbroiled beef to soothe a girl's hurt feelings. And if that failed, nestled in her fridge, she had some cheesecake smothered in a caramel sauce as backup.

"You're being deliberately obtuse. You can't use my stuff as fuel."

"Prove it. Looks like hot coals to me." Indeed, while they'd talked, his prized possessions were reduced to indistinguishable lumps. Using oven mitts, Tammy placed a metal grill over the glowing embers. With a deliberate, and admittedly taunting, grin in his direction, she grasped the steak with some tongs and slapped it on. *Mmm, nothing like hearing that sizzle.* "I'd invite you to stay, but as you can see, there's only enough for one, and besides, you made it quite clear this afternoon you don't like eating cows. Too fatty. So why don't you scurry off and visit your little stork of a girlfriend."

"She's not my girlfriend. We just hooked up for sex. You know full well I've got nowhere to stay."

"Not my problem. The townhouse is in my name as is the mortgage. Seeing as how we never had a rental agreement and we're no longer a couple, that makes you a trespasser. An unwelcome one. Now, leave before *I* call the cops."

"You can't just kick me out. What about my stuff?"

"The rest of your junk is on the front porch. You probably walked right past those trash bags on your way in. Take them when you leave, or tomorrow night, I'm having flame-kissed kebobs." Yummy. Marinated chicken chunks with red and green peppers over some spicy, pan-fried noodles.

She derived a certain satisfaction in watching the muscles in his jaw work. Not an impressive jaw as they went, kind of like the rest of him. What could she say? She'd foolishly fallen for his false charm and lies. Story of her life. A story she kept repeating. At least now Tammy no longer cried when they disappointed her and broke her heart. She got even.

"You're not just a fat, lousy lay, you're a nutjob. No man will ever want you," the jerk snapped as he stomped back through her house.

Maybe. But Tammy wasn't about to change herself. If fate meant for her to live a life alone, then so be it. There was always ice cream and Netflix to fall back on.

Chapter Two

"What the hell do you mean we lost another shipment?" Reid's bellow didn't quite shake the walls of his office, but it was close. His desk didn't fare so well when he slammed his fist down, leaving a dent in its already abused surface.

His second-in-command didn't flinch, but Brody did grimace. "I hate to say it, but it looks like we're being targeted."

"Gee, do you think?" was Reid's sarcastic reply. "The question is, by who? Who is dumb enough to screw with us?" *Make that screw with me.* His temper and general take-no-shit attitude was known far and wide amongst humans and shifters alike. It would take an idiot with large balls—big goddamned hairy ones—and a little brain to fuck with him. Reid didn't always play by the rules. Actually, he usually made them, and heck, sometimes even he didn't obey them.

As leader of his clan, Reid's word was law. His fist was justice. And his bellow meant run, because if he caught you... Let's just say, in the shifter world, justice was often quick, painful and at times, final. Reid had no patience for excuses, and no mercy for idiots.

However, it seemed someone either didn't know of his reputation or ignored it. That or they were positioning themselves to challenge him. *Bring it.* He might not like the paperwork duties that came with leading a mixed clan, but he'd be damned if he'd let some sneaky asshole waltz in and take it from him.

"No one's yet stepped forward to claim responsibility. But, given only our transport trucks have been targeted, I'd say it's deliberate, and they're not being gentle about it. We're missing three drivers now, not clan residents but transient workers. Three loads vanished into thin air and not one fucking witness," Brody added.

What Brody didn't say aloud was that, given they found blood staining the ground at the last registered satellite locations of the vehicles, the likelihood of the drivers still being alive was slim to none. The fact that whoever made their move didn't care if lives were lost proved troubling. Stealing and poaching was one thing. Reid and the other clans who chose to live in the Alaskan wilds had done it for decades, maybe even centuries. Hard to tell since they didn't keep any written accounts. But while they did have a few epic clashes, usually over territories or women—which he couldn't grasp, no honey pot was worth that kind of trouble—casualties were usually a result of a face-to-face battle, not coldly calculated ambushes. There was no honor in those.

Then again there would be little honor but a lot of screaming when he got his paws on the bastard responsible and squeezed his skull into a pulpy mush. As alpha of his clan, he'd get to decide on the justice. *Fuck with me and I'll destroy you.*

Reid drummed his fingers on his desktop. "When is our next run due to come in?"

"Couple of days. Travis is bringing in a load of supplies then loading up again with whatever the mine's got for us to haul out. With the loss of the last shipment, our partners down south are bitching."

"Because it's our fault we got hijacked." Reid couldn't help his sarcastic growl. While he might control who lived in his town, shifters and a few humans in on the secret, the outside world was another thing. Doing business with only his kind wasn't an option, which meant that explaining to human CEOs that a rival was poaching and planning a hostile takeover of his town wasn't a viable excuse. His buyers didn't want sob stories; they wanted what they ordered whether it be coal, fish or lumber. Goods he planned to deliver. Deliveries he needed for money, which he turned around and used to buy supplies for the clan. Supplies that had also gone missing, which meant there was going to be some grumbling soon, mostly by him if he didn't get to replenish his brown sugar stash. Fuck his cousins and their honey. Reid's sweet tooth ran towards brown sugar and maple syrup.

"Get me a map of the route. I want some of our men positioned at the more obvious ambush spots and watching. If there's another attack, I want someone to see who's leading it and report back." Because something about the whole thing stank. The fact that the drivers didn't belong to the clan was a glaring suspicion. Had Reid harbored criminals in his midst? But why wait so long to steal?

Jonathon, missing with the first truck, had worked as a driver for the company for almost fifteen months now. Steven for six. Only the last missing driver had spent less than a month in his position.

Were the missing trucks part of a planned heist engineered from the inside? Yes, they'd found blood at the scenes, but it wasn't too farfetched to wonder if someone planted it to throw them off the trail.

That was where the watching men came in. If this were the work of some transients, Travis wouldn't run into any problems during his run. If, however, an outside force truly was looking to undermine his power base, then Reid wanted to know.

"I'll have them in position well before the truck's expected to run past. What about engaging if Travis is attacked?"

"If they can help, then by all means they'd better get their furry asses into gear right quick. Better yet, send them out armed."

"What if Travis is hit out of range?"

"Think he'd listen to an order to tuck tail and run?"

Brody snorted.

"Yeah, that's what I thought. Stupid hotheaded cub. I'll make sure he's armed and stress caution. Hopefully, he'll use common sense and run if the numbers are against him. Then again, knowing my dumb-ass cousin, he'll attack no matter the odds, which is why I want him paired with Boris. But do it on the down low. Have Boris sneak on board and stay out of sight in the sleeper so if anyone's watching they don't know about him."

"Boris? That crazy fucker? You want to put him in a confined space with Travis? Do you hate your cousin that much?"

A smile was his reply. Boris might not play with a full deck, not since his return from overseas, but he was dependable. And deadly.

"Boris it is," Brody said with a shake of his head. "I'll give him a shout."

"No. I will." Putting Boris anywhere close to a fight was guaranteeing bloodshed. Reid wanted to stress the importance of keeping one of the thieves alive for questioning.

"And I'll warn Travis to behave. In other words, try and stay on Boris's good side, especially if he prefers to keep all his body parts intact."

Boris didn't suffer idiots, one of the reasons Reid liked him so much. He'd also trust the man with his life. "Can you think of anyone better though to have my cousin's back?" Other than Reid, who would ensure he also manned part of the return route in case trouble came knocking. He could use some stress relief and nothing worked better than dishing out violence. "Besides, maybe it's time we hit back. Showed them we're onto their game and not about to give in." Because no way was he explaining to his Aunt Betty-Sue why her one and only son, Travis, got killed or went missing when he could have stopped it.

That woman wielded a mean wooden spoon.

Chapter Three

When her boss told her she would be traveling to a remote part of Alaska, Tammy had no problem imagining a small rustic town, something picturesque with log cabins, big pine trees, a quaint general store, and a big moose wandering through town. Or wait, was she thinking of Canada?

No matter. What she'd not counted on when her plane landed was that the only way to get to Kodiak Point this time of the year—the heart of winter when night pretty much lasted something like twenty hours a day—was by hitching a ride.

Forget renting a car and driving. Not only was she refused by the agencies she queried, but some outright laughed.

"No way you're making it there alone. You're talking about the northern wilds. We don't let tourists drive up there by themselves. Not unless you don't mind your body being found when shit thaws in the spring."

Not exactly the most encouraging thing she'd ever heard. However, the insurance company she worked for insisted on sending her out in the field. Three separate claims involving trucks and entire trailers full of goods missing, and signs of foul play against the drivers, meant someone needed to investigate the business profiting from the so-called incidents, especially when her agency's attempts to question were stonewalled by the owner of the company, whose answer for everything was a vague, "Read the state trooper report."

She'd read the bare-bones report. What a joke. No suspects. No clues. No evidence other than bloodstains and three tractor trailers vanished into seemingly thin air. Accidents happened, especially in harsh conditions. Could they have slid off the road and sunk under some ice? Gotten lost in a whiteout? Gotten beamed up by aliens?

Sure. It was possible. But three in less than a month? All traveling to and from the same town? All for the same company? Add in the fact that they vanished into seemingly thin air. That smelled like fraud.

So there she was at the airport, arguing with the car rental place that point-blank refused, but snidely suggested she look into catching a ride on a dog sled.

Not happening. Nor was she clinging to some stranger on the back of a snowmobile. A resourceful employee, Tammy had a better idea.

Bright and early the following morning, Tammy stood in the loading dock area at the warehouse where Kodiak Point got its grocery supplies. She leaned against a blue big rig wearing her brand-new, red parka and knee-high moon boots, new because it seemed an Alaskan winter was on a whole different level from the winters she was accustomed to. Cozy in her new gear, she held her post until a tall fellow appeared, the exterior lights of the truck yard illuminating his approach. Eight a.m. and still no dawn. Ugh. She wasn't sure how Alaskan residents handled all this infernal darkness.

The guy stopped in front of her. He grinned, a toothpaste-white smile as he said, "Good morning. Can I help you?" Given his handsome looks, which comprised a square jaw and dirty blond hair with a hank that kept falling over his eyes, she could just imagine the ladies loved him. But given he was probably about five or more years younger than her, and a sure skirt chaser, his charm failed to melt her.

"You most certainly can help me. My name is Tamara Roberts, and I'm here on behalf of…" As she launched into her spiel about who she worked for, and why she waited by his truck, the genial smile on the fellow's face shrank. He let her speak her piece, but when she finished her speech with, "which is why I'll be catching a ride with you," he finally interrupted.

"You want me to take you with me?" He didn't even try to couch his shocked tone.

"Yes." She'd already elaborated on the reasons why and saw no reason to repeat herself.

"But I'm a transport truck, not a taxi."

"I understand that. However, there is no other means it seems at the moment of reaching your town or company, other than the obvious. By truck. A truck route, I might add, that I was sent out here to investigate. So unless you have something to hide—"

"Of course not."

"Then I don't see the problem. You're already going to Kodiak Point. I need to get there and observe your business at work. Seems like a win-win situation to me."

Apparently he didn't perceive it in the same light. "I need to call my boss."

"Going to warn him? Maybe call off plans to have this truck *mysteriously*," she added finger quotes for emphasis, "disappear."

"Are you calling me a thief?" His brows soared with incredulity.

She shrugged. "I don't know yet. That's what I'm here to find out. But your arguments are making you look pretty suspicious."

"And I'm beginning to think you're nuts, lady."

Familiar words. "Join the crowd. So, what's it going to be? Are you taking me, or am I calling my boss at head office and letting them know that your company is impeding my investigation?" *Please let him agree.* She didn't need him calling her bluff. Her boss had no idea of the troubles she was having, and she preferred it stayed that way lest he think she was complaining. She had her eye on a position opening up that would entail better cases and more money. If she could succeed in proving fraud and preventing a payout, it would earn her some major brownie points.

The guy scrubbed a hand through his hair, making it stand on end. "I guess I'm taking you with me. But I warn you, there's no pit stops on the way. If you've got to pee, then you're doing it in a cup, and if you're hungry, you'd better have food. Once we hit the road, we don't stop until we get there."

An almost eight hour drive. Double ugh. "Don't worry about me. I've got the bladder of a camel."

"And the boss has the temper of a bear," the young guy mumbled as he wandered away, logbook in hand to perform his circle check on the truck.

Tammy didn't release her sigh of relief until the guy rounded the corner of the truck, checking things off his list. She'd not been sure her ploy would work. Sure, it seemed like the best plan at the time, but when it came to actually implementing it, she'd harbored some misgivings.

The idea of riding with a stranger admittedly worried her a touch. When she'd told her mother this morning as she packed her toiletries before checking out of the motel, phone tucked between her ear and shoulder, her mother had done her best to plant all kinds of doubt.

"You're going to be alone with this man for how long in that truck? Are you out of your mind, Tamara Sophie Roberts! God only knows how long since he's seen a woman."

"Probably not as long since I've been with a man," she muttered, shoving a pair of brand-new woolly socks into an open crevice. Since her flaming breakup, she'd stayed away from the opposite sex, not out of depression or heartache, but more because she was tired of dealing with the bullshit.

She'd really thought Asshat, her last boyfriend, was the one. Or at least she tolerated him well enough to try and live with him. However, it was as if that closeness was the trigger that turned him from all right boyfriend into douchebag. It didn't take long once he moved in before the snide remarks about her eating habits began. Then came the hints, which got less and less subtle, about her needing to lose weight and exercise more. But, for the sake of trying to make things work, she'd tolerated his annoying litany—until she caught him cheating.

Speaking of annoying, her mother wasn't done.

"The situation isn't funny, Tammy. A young lady shouldn't travel alone with a stranger. What if he decides to take advantage of you? Or the truck slides off the road? I've been watching that ice trucking show with your father. Do you know how dangerous it is?"

"First off, Mom, no one's taking advantage of me." Unless she felt like it. "And second, the whole reason I'm out here is to investigate why their trucks are having so many incidents." Which, on second thought, kind of lent credence to her mom's argument.

Hmm. Better not dwell on that aspect. She'd have to trust those she investigated wouldn't sabotage a delivery with her aboard. That was sure to raise even more flags with her insurance company.

And so went that conversation for an irritatingly long half hour. In the end, Tammy prevailed, mostly because she hung up when her mother launched into her theory that the Northern Lights were some kind of nuclear radiation that would affect Tammy's eggs and mess up her chance to have a baby.

The fact that Tammy needed a man to make the baby wasn't something her irrational mother bothered to factor in, and if the Northern Lights were indeed some leftover radioactive waste from crashed aliens, then Tammy could only hope she'd end up with some cool superpower, like one to spot assholes and run the other way.

The driver came back into view, still ticking away at his checklist, and having gotten her way, Tammy decided it was time to play nice.

"So you know who I am, but you've yet to give me your name."

Actually, she knew who he was, Travis Huntley, cousin to the owner of Beark Enterprises. Knowing he was related in some fashion to the owner, and main suspect, was, in a sense, a relief. What were the chances they'd sabotage a truck with a family member aboard?

"I'm Travis."

"Sorry if we got off on the wrong foot, Travis."

He chuckled. "You just took me by surprise. If you're that determined to get to Kodiak Point, then I'll take you. But once you get there, you're on your own with my boss."

"Your boss being Reid Carver?"

"That's right. And he doesn't like surprises."

"You know him well then?"

"I sure do considering he's my cousin, which is why I'm warning you right now, he's not going to like the fact you didn't give him notice you were coming."

"Does your cousin have something to hide?"

If she hadn't been watching his face, she might have missed it—a guarded look, there one second, gone the next. He hid the fleeting glimpse with a bright smile, showing off impressive canines. "Reid, hiding something? Nope. He's exactly what he appears to be. A big ol' bear with a loud roar and I'm-the-alpha attitude." For some reason, Travis seemed to find his words amusing, or so she judged by his smirk as he finished his routine check of the truck.

Having read up on the whole trucking thing on her flight over—a flight made longer by the lack of decent food—she understood it was mandatory that all drivers perform a visual inspection of their vehicle every time they left on a run. Lights, tires, hydraulics, even the oil levels and other fluids, as well as any scratches or dents, were supposed to be reported in their log. All part of reducing the number of accidents and ensuring fleets were maintained and not posing a safety hazard to not only the drivers but also others sharing the road.

Checkmark in his favor, he'd done it, but was it his usual practice or something he'd just done because of her presence? She'd have to get her hands on his logbook for a peek later.

"Is that your stuff?" he asked, inclining his head toward her pile of luggage—two suitcases and a satchel purse.

She nodded.

"I'll toss it in the sleeper."

"Is that where I'll be sitting for the trip?"

"Not unless you like to share. Boris is back there sleeping, and he's not a dude you want to wake up."

Advice Travis didn't seem to heed. He'd no sooner seen her seated than he clambered in on his side, then he heaved her luggage through the opening to the back.

"What the fuck?" grumbled a voice. "Are you that determined to die young, cub?"

"Watch your language, Boris. We've got a lady on board."

A grizzled face poked between the dark curtains covering the back. "Since when are the girls you pick up, 'ladies'?"

Tammy bit her lip as Travis frowned. "Are you implying something?"

"No, I'm outright stating."

She dove in to his rescue. "I'm not one of Travis' lady friends. I'm here representing the insurance bureau, investigating the recent spate of accidents your company has been having."

Her announcement met with a grunt, and Boris fixed Travis with a stare. "Does Reid know?"

Travis shook his head.

"Your funeral." With a snort, Boris disappeared into the back.

"Pleasant fellow," she remarked as Travis put the truck into gear.

"Boris? Bah. He's just a big old moose. I'm actually surprised we got that much out of him. The man thinks grunting is a language. But he's a good guy, deep down inside. Real deep," he added in a slightly louder voice.

As if to give credence to Travis' words, a louder grunt emerged from the back.

Tammy couldn't help but hear her mother's words repeat. Not just alone with one man, but two. *Please don't let the newspaper read Too-stupid-to-live insurance investigator's body was found...* Nope. She refused to give in to her mother's crazy paranoia and trusted her gut, and her gut said she had nothing to fear from these two.

Especially not-talkative Travis, who, despite his initial protest about taking her, now seemed determined to make the best of it. Given his loquacious nature, she thought it prudent to furtively question him about his boss and company.

"So how long have you been working for your cousin?"

"Since high school. The whole town pretty much does. Without the company we'd have no jobs. Even the general store would probably fold without it."

"Your main export is coal?"

"Coal, some precious metals if the miners come across them. We do have a small fishing fleet, but a lot of that stuff gets sold or traded locally. And we also deal in timber."

"Your trucks, which transport these goods out, are also the main means of bringing stuff in as well."

"Yes. Without these regular runs, lots of families would have to travel hours for the basics. Reid came up with a system where we time our distribution drop-offs with pick-ups."

"Sounds like an efficient businessman, your cousin."

"He is."

"What does he think of the trucks that have gone missing?"

"Despite what you might suspect, or how it looks, he's not behind the disappearances. Reid cares too much about our town and the people to screw them like that."

"Even you have to admit it's kind of suspicious. I mean, come on, three trucks?"

Travis' knuckles turned white where he gripped the wheel. "One was driven by a friend of mine. A missing friend, whose girlfriend is expecting their first child. Trust me when I say, we had nothing to do with this. No one from our town would stoop so low."

"Then who would?" Tammy realized the oddness of her question, and yet, if these weren't strokes of bad luck and someone was causing them, then why? Was it a rival company? That would make no sense. Why attack people and deliveries when someone could throw a monkey wrench in the operation by calling the ministry of labor, or the eco nuts? If either found a hint of impropriety, they could shut down operations with a few simple phone calls.

Whatever the real reason, Travis turned uncommunicative, and Tammy pulled out the claim to read it over again. They had a long drive ahead, and she wanted to know everything she could about the case.

Hours later, she was ready to shred the paperwork. Boring and not imparting anything she didn't already know, all it seemed capable of managing was putting her to sleep, which, given her poor sleep in the motel—Johnny and Susan weren't quiet in their mutual enthusiasm for each other—might not be a bad idea. The few hours of daylight this part of Alaska got came and went too quickly, leaving them in a pressing darkness she didn't enjoy at all.

Since Boris didn't seem inclined to give up his berth, and she wasn't about to insist, she did her best to make herself comfortable in the front seat and nap. Easier than expected given the never-ending dull vista, lit only by the headlights, which did little more than illuminate the swath of coniferous trees lining the ice- and snow-covered route. Lulled by the engine and shadows, she slept.

The jolt alone wasn't what woke her, the route had plenty of those, but the slowing down of the truck, which trembled until they came to a standstill, did.

Eyes grainy with sleep, she rubbed her face and around a yawn asked, "Why are we stopped? Are we there yet?" Or was this where her mother's prediction came true and Travis turned into a wild mountain man determined to have his way with her while Boris grunted on the sidelines, waiting his turn.

"We seem to have a flat tire," Travis announced.

"From what?" she muttered. An icicle? But given their location—the middle of nowhere—the better question was, "How do you fix it?"

"Not easily. If you'll excuse me, I'm going to call it in."

Without even zipping up his coat, Travis hopped out of the truck, the sudden swirling chill of the outdoors whipping through the cab and making her shiver. Its briskness also stole the question on the tip of her tongue. *Why is he going out there to call?* Odd, because he had a perfectly good CB system in the cab, where it was warm and illuminated. And yes, not so scary.

She couldn't stop a shiver, whether from cold or the dark unknown outside the windows. Tammy zipped up the parka she'd not entirely removed, her driver apparently preferring a cool cab to a toasty heated one. The downy softness did not dispel the chill of foreboding, however.

How long would it take for a tow truck to show up and help change the tire? Should she call her mom on her satellite phone—and listen to her 'I told you so'? Should she panic because of the ululation of wolves that started outside, an eerie sound that raised every hair on her body? Suddenly the reports of blood found made a lot more sense. If the drivers got dumped from their trucks, how long would they last without shelter or a weapon? Gulp. Welcome to the great outdoors.

Of more concern, where the hell was Travis? He'd jumped out of the truck to make his call, but peering out of the windows, snow and shadows made visibility impossible. She couldn't spot him. "This is not happening," she muttered, especially considering she was weaponless. Given the tighter rules since 9/11, she'd not even tried to bring her registered gun with her on the flight. She'd figured she could always pick one up somewhere once she arrived. She would have, if she'd had time. *Time I should have made,* she thought with a shiver as the howls seemed to get closer.

Either the approaching wildlife or their lack of motion roused the man in the back. Boris poked a grizzled head from the gap in the curtains. "What's happening? Why are we stopped?"

"Flat tire."

"Where's Travis?"

"Outside somewhere. Which might not be a good place for him." She pointed to the yellow eyes emerging from the gloom. Wolves. Quite a few of them, and look, she finally got an answer as to where Travis was. In the glow of the truck's headlights, Travis appeared, tucking his phone into his pocket, and while his lips moved, she couldn't tell what he said.

Boris cursed under his breath. "I should go help."

"Help? Are you out of your mind? For that matter, is Travis out of his? We are safer staying in this truck. Wolves or not, they can't open doors or chew through metal. If we stay in the cab, we'll remain safe."

"Good plan. You stay in the truck." Boris wedged his massive shoulders sideways in an attempt to squeeze into the front.

She would have asked Boris where he thought he was going and what exactly he thought he could do, but a more disturbing thing was happening. She leaned forward. "Why is Travis taking off his coat? And his boots. Is he seriously stripping?" Her voice grew more and more shrill as the situation went from weird to extremely disturbing.

"See, this is why I won't ever get married. Women! Always asking questions," grumbled Boris. He pulled back behind the curtain, and she heard him rummaging.

"What are you doing?" she asked.

"What needs to be done. Sleep, little human."

Sleep? Was this man as lunatic as his partner? A prick on the side of her neck saw that thought and all others sliding away as she slumped into darkness.

Chapter Four

It just so happened, according to satellite co-ordinates, that Reid was close by when the call from Travis arrived. He'd not meant to head out so far, but his gut—and his bear—insisted he ride parallel to the route his next delivery would arrive from. If there was one thing Reid had learned when he served overseas, it was to listen to his instincts. If they screamed he would probably be needed, then he heeded the warning.

"What is it, Trav?"

"Boss, we've got a problem. A couple actually. The most pressing is I got a flat tire."

"From what?"

"Nothing I could see."

"So, in other words, you don't know if it's intentional or not."

"Nope. But I'm gonna need help."

"With the tire? You know how to change a tire. You've got Boris to give you a hand." Between the two of them, they had enough muscle to handle it.

"The flat is not the problem nor are the wolves."

Reid straightened his spine. "Wolves? Shifters or wild ones?"

"Given their tiny size, I'd say wild ones, but they look hungry."

They always were this time of the year. "So take care of them."

"I plan to. It's the human I'm not sure what to do with."

Those words caused Reid to practically fall off his snowmobile as he barked, "Human? What fucking human, and what the hell is he doing in your truck?"

"First off, he is a she, and she didn't give me much of a choice when she showed up this morning in the truck yard."

As Travis quickly relayed who she was and why she rode with him, Reid's irritation swelled. He'd expected some kind of insurance investigator to show up at one point, a human he had no way of diverting. Damn his insurance company. But he'd at least expected some kind of warning. Getting ambushed like this didn't sit well with him at all.

Unfortunately, while he could control who moved into the town he ruled, he couldn't control outside forces, and the need for insurance to run a business was one of them. Usually Reid would have swallowed the cost of a lost truck and not reported it, but with three missing, and foul play suspected against the drivers? Three was too many even for him to hide. Not to mention he couldn't quite absorb or eliminate it from the ledgers cost-wise, not without drawing even more unwanted attention. The IRS gave no one any quarter.

Reid had to make a snap decision. "Forget what I said before. Don't do anything. We can't risk this broad suspecting what you are. I'll send a team to help with the tire."

"What about the wolves?"

"Ignore them. They should scatter when the others arrive on their sleds." Reid included himself among that number. Sometimes just the scent of his bestial side was enough to send unenlightened creatures running. True shifters on the other hand? They always knew to run when he showed up sporting a scowl.

"Ignore the wolves? Yeah, I don't think that's an option."

"Travis!" Reid growled his cousin's name. "There is a human watching. Get in the truck and play cool."

"Ah, come on, cuz. That's no fun."

"No fun is letting the girl know what we are."

"No, no fun is letting her get eaten." Travis' tone turned from mocking to serious. "Remember what I said about the wolves not being shifters?"

"Yeah."

"Well, apparently I spoke too soon. Their alpha just showed up, and he's definitely not run-of-the-mill. Gotta go."

Before Reid could yell at him, the phone went dead, and Reid almost sent it flying off into the woods. But he reined in his temper. He needed the co-ordinates of Travis' location. Punching them into the GPS of his snowmobile, it showed him less than four miles from his cousin.

Only minutes at top speed on his sled. Minutes that could cost Travis his life—and impact Reid's.

His Aunt Betty-Sue would skin him if her boy didn't make it back to town in one piece.

Throttle open all the way, and his RPM in the flashy red, Reid sped to the rescue. The rumble of his engine hid the sound of battle as he approached the area, but he saw the headlights of the truck long before that. Ditching his machine, Reid stripped quickly, his clothing specially made to allow for a rapid shed. Only dumb shifters with money to burn ripped through their wardrobe.

Bones cracked and reformed as Reid took off running. He hit the ground on four paws, claws digging into the icy surface for purchase, his shivering human skin disappearing under a layer of thick, brown fur. When he opened his mouth, now full of sharp teeth, his roar echoed and declared to all that he'd arrived, a fact he didn't give the wolves time to digest before he bowled into them, massive paws slashing.

In the heat of battle it was difficult to really perceive individual events. Everything happened in a blur of sound, motion, and snatched glimpses. Reid took in the action in snapshot glances. There was a grizzly, his cousin, with a wolf hanging off his side, its teeth clamped while Travis held another in a hug, their snapping jaws fighting for the killing blow.

Furry, snarling shapes lunged and dove. Some of them thought to gang up on Reid, but it would take more than a few mangy gray wolves to worry him. If this had been a pack of true werewolves though, then he would have really had a good time. Wild and puny, normal ones, though? Piece of decadent maple pie.

Reid tore into them, the coppery taste of blood warm on his tongue. While he might have balked in his human shape at the flavor, his beast reveled in it. He ruled these parts. He protected his clan. And these scurvy curs would feel his wrath.

His breath puffed out, a white steam from his nostrils, as he waded into battle, determined to teach them all a lesson, a fatal one. At the edge of his vision, he caught a glimpse of antlers. Boris, his massive moose frame trampling the wolves nagging his hocks while he tossed his head, his wide rack of antlers banging about the large wolf snarling at him.

Aha, the leader.

Ignoring those still snapping for his attention, Reid lumbered toward Boris and the shifter who was obviously in charge of this attack. He bellowed a challenge, expecting the alpha wolf to meet him. After all, the bastard had the balls to attack his truck and his people. If a run for leadership of his clan was what he wanted, then Reid would oblige. But the yellow-bellied coward didn't turn to face him. With a sharp yip, the large wolf turned tail and ran.

What the fuck?

Reid almost chased after. His Kodiak certainly wanted to, but common sense prevailed. Travis, barely more than a cub really, let adrenaline dictate his actions and would have raced after the shifter, but Boris stepped in his path and grunted. Funny how, whether man or beast, he sounded pretty much the same.

When Travis moved to get around the towering moose, Boris shifted to block him again. As the ululations of the fleeing wolves faded, Travis swapped to his human form and yelled,

"What the fuck? Why aren't we chasing these bastards?"

Taking his human shape in the cold was something even a big ol' bear like Reid never quite got used to. Human skin, even that of a shifter, wasn't meant for the harsh winter climate, not without a few thermal layers. He didn't reply to Travis' tirade but directed his question to Boris. "The human female, where is she?"

Boris, who'd also shifted and stretched his massive shape, marked in knotted scars, replied, "Sleeping. I tranquilized her before the fight began. She didn't see anything."

At least Boris showed good sense. All of Reid's trucks had tranquilizer darts, a just-in-case that served them better than guns and bullets, especially when they needed to capture someone and question them, or if a shifter got drunk in town and needed some sedating. Alcohol didn't just loosen inhibitions and tongues. It sometimes gave rise to the beast within.

The cold did its best to steal his heat as he strode back to his snowmobile and his pile of clothes. Making sure he'd wiped most of the blood off his skin first, he then calmly dressed while Travis, still yelling, finally gave in to the climate and put back on his own garments.

Straddling his sled, Reid gave it a bit of gas and brought it alongside the truck. He let it idle as he regarded his cousin, who huffed and puffed, still irritated but quiet at last.

"Are you done having a temper tantrum?" Reid asked in a low tone.

Travis opened his mouth—must have seen something on Reid's face—and shut it in favor of nodding his head.

"Good. First off. If you ever disobey a direct order from me again, family or not, I'm going to beat your ass until you can't fucking sit for a week. I told you to get in the goddamned truck and wait for me."

"We were under attack."

"And you jumped in, without waiting for backup and without thinking. What if there'd been guys with guns in the woods? Or more shifters?"

"There wasn't, and I had Boris with me."

"Not the point, there could have been. And what about the human?"

"She's sleeping."

"Did you know that before you stripped down and went grizzly?"

His sheepish expression and hanging head said it all.

"Stupid. Unbelievably stupid."

The boy didn't know when to quit while he was still in one piece. His sullen expression took on an angry edge as he retorted, "So what was I supposed to do? Lock the doors and pretend they weren't there?"

"Yes. That would have worked. Maybe screamed and freaked out a little with the human girl. It's what a normal person does. Instead, you were stupid, and we had to take desperate measures." Well, not so much desperate as difficult to explain. Now Reid would have to think of a lie to feed the woman when she woke up.

"As stupid as letting them get away? Why the hell didn't you let me chase them down?" Travis still wouldn't admit he was wrong. Young fool.

Reid's brows arched. "Do you really have to ask why? Let me see. Waddle off in the dark after a werewolf and his pack, who, for all you know, was part of a larger group. Leave the truck, the trailer, not to mention a human unguarded, again without knowing if there was another larger group waiting in the shadows. And, oh, the most obvious reason, because you wouldn't have caught them. You might be fast on four feet, cousin, but you're not that fast."

With each verbal strike from Reid, Travis' mutinous expression sobered, and it was a very meek grizzly who said, "Sorry, Reid. I didn't think of any of that."

"Of course you didn't," Boris announced with a slap on the boy's back that almost sent him flying. "That's why Reid here's the leader of our clan and not any of us pea-brained minions."

Reid snorted. "Minion? Really?"

"Should I have gone with henchmen instead?" asked the normally taciturn man, surprising him with his question. Someone was in a good mood, probably because he'd gotten to fight. Boris' sly grin almost drew one from Reid.

"How about we don't call the folk I'm trying to lead anything." Except pains in his ass when they wouldn't listen.

"I'm going to get the tools to change the tire."

"I'll help," Travis volunteered.

"I guess I should check on the human," Reid added with a grimace. At least Boris had the good sense to put her to sleep, although how he'd explain away her sudden slumber he didn't have a clue.

The passenger side door wasn't locked and when Reid opened it, he managed to get his arms up just in time to catch the woman who tumbled out. At least he assumed there was a woman somewhere within the thick red parka. Hard to tell with all the padding in the way.

A vanilla scent tickled his nose, a womanly smell that perked his inner bear's interest. It gave a happy rumble, but Reid didn't pay him much mind, given he also made the same sound when his grandmother made her famous pot roast with thick, pan gravy. Still ... he'd never had his bear think a human smelled delicious before. *No eating people.* The first rule a shifter learned, right after don't lick the electrical outlet.

As Reid held her limp frame with one arm, curiosity had him pushing back the curly hair covering her face with his gloved fingers. Human or not, she was cute, just not what the media would call gorgeous. She did, however, appeal to him with her faint freckles splashed across the bridge of her nose. He even liked her snub nose, rounded cheeks, and tiny rosebud of a mouth. She possessed smooth skin and thick lashes, which brushed her pale cheeks as she slept, making him wonder what color her eyes were.

Hefting her into his arms, he noted she was a woman with a bit of weight to her, some meat on her bones—which the bear in him heartily approved of. A man his size didn't find scrawny waifs appealing. A full handful and something to bury himself into was more to his taste.

But speaking of appealing, why the hell was he appraising her this way? The human was here to investigate him and his company. She was not dating material. Not even close, even if his bear liked the smell of her.

Carrying her around the side of the truck, he caught Travis and Boris spreading out the needed tools to get the vehicle moving again. In the distance, he could hear the hum of approaching snowmobiles. Reinforcements arrived, and no, he wasn't guessing. He'd recognized the distinct "Yahoo!" Brody hollered as a greeting.

"The boys are arriving, which means I'm leaving."

"You taking her with you?" Boris asked.

Peering down into her face, Reid couldn't have said what prompted him to say, "Yes. The sooner I get her to Kodiak Point, the safer she'll be."

If Boris and Travis saw the illogic in his statement, they didn't voice it aloud. A good thing too because Reid would have been hard-pressed to explain how he, alone on a snowmobile, toting an unconscious human, just over two hours out from town, with who knew what in his way, was safer than having her finish the ride in the truck with a crew of his men.

His decision didn't make sense on the surface, but that didn't stop him from grabbing a bungee cord from the tool kit, strapping her to his chest, face tucked into him, legs straddling his, and heading for home on his sled.

And once there, he really couldn't have explained why instead of bringing her to the mini motel in town, he brought her to his house. Not his bed, mind you, but given he gave her the room right across the hall, not far.

He did draw the line at stripping her out of her clothes. More because his grandmother, who lived with him, shooed him from the room, stating, "Get out, you mangy furball, while I make her comfortable."

"Why can't I help you?"

Lips set in a tight line, his grandmother huffed, "Because it's not proper."

Given his thoughts when he saw her peeled from her bulky jacket to reveal a very womanly shape, Reid could only agree. Despite her humanity and general unsuitableness, the ideas running through his head weren't decent at all.

But really, did his grandmother have to shove him out the door and then slam it shut?

Chapter Five

Waking in a strange bed, Tammy stretched and didn't panic until she remembered her last moments before sleep.

Wolves!

Panic infused, she scrambled to a sitting position. The fog in her mind cleared fast, and she quickly noted that not only were there no wolves in sight, but that she seemed whole of body—although her mind remained debatable. One odd thing though was she wore only her T-shirt and long johns.

Someone stripped her!

Someone brought her here, although where here was she didn't have a clue.

And someone drugged her.

Um, yeah, that last part kind of trumped all the rest.

Placing her bare feet on a rug beside the bed, she took a better look around. *I am in a bedroom.* A brilliant observation given the double bed with brass head rail, wooden night stand, straight-back chair draped with her missing clothes, and a tall wooden dresser, which had a kerosene lantern sitting atop it and a carved figurine of a bear standing on its hind paws, snarling. The walls were timber, not plaster, smooth wood logs with the cracks in between filled. If she were to guess, she was in someone's home, but whose?

The first door she opened led to a closet with only empty hangars. The next door she tried to a washroom. Locking it behind her, she made use of the toilet and then the sink to splash water on her face. Only as she patted her skin dry did she take a peek at her reflection. Freckles, messy hair, and perky nose; check. No sign of attack.

She took stock of her other body parts, running hands over her frame, noting that she was still wearing the same bra, panties, and sexy long johns she'd picked up in the men's section at Walmart. It relieved her to note no evidence of soreness in any of her girly places.

It didn't seem she'd suffered any kind of assault. So what happened? She knew her sleep wasn't a natural one, but why exactly had Boris—had to be since she distinctly remembered Travis outside the truck stripping, which was a whole other weirdness—drugged her? Was he part of the truck sabotage, trailer-stealing ring?

A ton of questions, and yet none would get answered while she stared at her reflection. Exiting the bathroom, she ensured the door to the bedroom was locked before she stripped out of her long johns and other garments to put on fresh ones.

Then, sucking in a deep breath to calm her frazzled nerves, she went looking for answers—and her phone, which wasn't in any of the piles in the room. Then again, neither was her coat, boots, or purse.

Once again, she really wished she'd spent a day arming herself. *That's the last time I leave home without a gun.*

The door opened soundlessly, the hinges not making the slightest squeak, and she eased out into a shadowy hall lit only by the glow of light coming up some stairs. Her feet, clad in socks, didn't make a sound on the carpeted floor as she inched along, practically holding her breath, her ears straining to hear.

So when a low voice from behind her, said, "Going somewhere?" was it any wonder she screamed and did what any self-respecting city girl would do? She spun and swung.

Her closed fist hit a brick wall.

Ouch!

With a yelp, she drew her hand back and then stared at the chest she'd tried to smoke, less chest and more like impenetrable barrier. And a wide one at that.

Glancing upward, then up, up, and holy fuck, up some more, she caught the less-than-amused expression on the giant's face.

Way to go. Piss off the big, scary dude. "Um, hi?" she offered tentatively.

"If that's how you say hello to strangers, I'd hate to see how you say goodbye. Is it a city thing to hit your hosts?" he asked, his sarcasm evident.

"Only when the hosts have a nasty habit of sneaking up on women and scaring the pants off them," she retorted.

"Seeing as how you're still wearing your pants, and I was hardly sneaking, I have no idea what you're talking about."

His size, not to mention his attitude—bristly with a side of arrogant—threw her off kilter. Not enjoying the lack of control, and heart still pounding from fright, she went on the attack. "Who are you, and where am I?" she asked.

"I'm Reid Carver, and you're in my house."

The name rang a bell—a warning one. "You're the owner of Beark Enterprises, aren't you?"

He nodded.

"I'm here to investigate you." Nothing like putting it out there bluntly to see if she could catch him off guard.

It didn't work. His lips, which she now couldn't help but note were full and tempting, curled into an amused grin that went well with his square jaw and rugged features. Not exactly a cover-model man, but handsome, too handsome if you liked a man with a rough, slightly untamed look—who also happened to tower over her.

It wasn't often Tammy met a man who made her feel petite. Or who could heat her cheeks just by perusing her from the tips of her wooly socks to the top of her mop of curls.

"Do you mind not staring at me?" she asked as she crossed her arms over her chest.

"Why not? You've already stated your intent to investigate. It seems only fair I get to do the same."

"But I'm not the one possibly concealing something." Other than a penchant for chocolate bars and ice cream.

He held out his hands and spun for her. "By all means, inspect me. I've got nothing to hide."

Nothing except what she judged to be an excess of muscle. His plaid shirt stretched across ungodly wide shoulders while well-worn jeans hugged thick, corded thighs. If her mission involved finding a hot body, she'd succeeded, but she wasn't here on pleasure.

"What happened to the truck I was traveling in? Where's Travis and Boris? Why was I drugged? What happened to me while I was asleep? Why am I here? Where is here, and don't tell me your house again. Where's my phone? What—"

Under her barrage of questions, he held up a hand. "Slow down, woman."

"Woman?" A single brow of hers arched. "My name is Tamara Roberts, and I'm here on behalf of—"

He interrupted. "I know who you are and why you're here. To investigate me. And I understand you have questions, but could we conduct them one at a time, perhaps somewhere a little more comfortable than my upstairs hall?"

"I'm not going anywhere with you until I get my phone and put a call in to my office to let them know I've arrived." *And who I'm with in case they need a place to look for my body when I go missing.*

"I don't know where your phone is. Probably wherever my grandmother stashed your coat and stuff."

Excuses. Didn't that just figure? Before she could accuse him of anything, he pulled a phone out of his pocket and handed it to her. "Use mine."

Snatching it, she stowed her curiosity over the man who lived with his grandmother and immediately dialed her mother's number. She ignored him as she scampered down the steps, trying to put some distance between her and the giant. It didn't work too well, given she swore she could feel his eyes boring into her back, but at least he didn't attempt to stop her.

Her mother answered with a bright, "Hello."

"Mom, it's me."

"Tammy. It's about time you called." Her mother's relief was evident. "Whose phone are you calling from? Your information is showing as private caller."

"I just wanted to let you know I arrived safely," more or less, "and am currently at the house of Reid Carver."

"Isn't he the man you're investigating?"

"Not him, his company. Listen, I don't have time to talk right now." Nor the time to listen to her mother's tirade, especially if she heard about the wolves and everything else. "I just wanted to let you know I'm safe and I'll call you later."

"But—"

"Love you, Mom, bye."

She disconnected the call and whirled in the foyer, only to squeak as, once again, the behemoth managed to creep up on her.

"Would you stop doing that?"

"Doing what?" he asked with a smirk.

She eyed him suspiciously. He tried to look innocent, but failed. No one his size could hope to look anything but menacing, unless he was looking really menacing. "Oh never mind. We're out of the hall. Mind answering some questions now?"

"Not quite. We've just exchanged the upstairs hall for the main floor version. Follow me and we'll go somewhere there are actual stools and chairs. Or would you prefer to keep me standing as you harangue me with questions? Perhaps you want me to fetch you a bright light?"

Smartass. "I wouldn't call wanting answers haranguing," she grumbled as she followed his broad back through an archway into a massive kitchen lit by a multitude of recessed ceiling lights.

Holy culinary temple. For someone like Tammy, who had a healthy appetite and enjoyed the preparation of food as much as eating it, she practically drooled over the dreamy kitchen.

Cabinetry in a clear pine went floor to ceiling in a u-shape, with only the massive stainless steel stove—with more burners than the fire code surely allowed—and a fridge that was possibly larger than her walk-in closet at home—breaking up the huge amount of storage. A picture window over the sink reflected her gaping image back, and she snapped her mouth shut.

Given the luxury of the kitchen, the man was obviously loaded, and while his file didn't mention a significant other, that didn't mean he didn't cook or have someone who cooked for him. *Let's not forget, his business insurance just asks for his marital status. He could quite easily have a girlfriend and a half-dozen kids for all I know.* Although, if he did, she hoped their heads at least took after the mother. The thought of birthing one of his mutant and surely large progeny was enough to make any girl think twice about getting serious with him.

"Have a seat while I fix us something to eat," he offered, gesturing to a stool in front of the massive island topped in gray granite swirled with green.

Perching herself, she eyed him as he opened the massive two-door fridge and pulled out an array of containers and condiments. So he wasn't completely useless in the kitchen, good to know but not the most important thing right now despite her grumbling belly.

"Are you trying to stall me?" she asked.

Reid paused from his tomato slicing to fix her with a stare. "No. I'm hungry, and I'm betting you are too. It was a long trip. Feel free to grill me while I make us some sandwiches."

"Let's start with why your drivers drugged me." She came out with guns blasting and resisted an urge to cock her finger like a pistol and blow on the tip.

"Ah yes, an unfortunate incident. When Boris saw the wolves, he grabbed the tranquilizer gun we keep in all the trucks. For some reason, it was empty, and he fumbled the dart as he tried to load it. That unfortunate fumble saw you pricked."

"You're kidding, right?"

"Why on earth would I joke? You can ask anyone who knows me. I am not given to jesting."

"Who the hell keeps sleep darts in their trucks?" Other than pervs who couldn't get a date.

"In case you hadn't noticed, we live in a bit of an untamed area of the world, one where wild animals still roam far and wide. Given we prefer to preserve wildlife when possible, we have adopted certain methods, humanitarian methods, to problems our drivers might encounter on the road. Putting predators to sleep rather than killing them is a prime example."

"So what, he was going to zap all the wolves on the road?" She couldn't hide her incredulity.

Reid shrugged as he shredded some lettuce. "I don't see why you find that so incredible. And remember, Boris never actually saw how many there were. Hearing of the wolf situation, Boris meant to do well, but he'd just woken up and, still in a groggy state of mind, had a clumsy moment."

The man didn't deign to look at her as he calmly explained her drugging. Nope, cool as a cucumber, he sawed through a thick loaf of bread, so fresh still that the crust crackled and the most heavenly smell wafted forth, making Tammy's mouth water. Talk about not fighting fair.

"Let's say for a moment I believe your cockamamie story. How the heck do you explain Travis going to confront the wolves and stripping on the way?"

"Are you sure that's what he was doing?" Reid questioned as he slathered the bread with real butter then mayonnaise, atop which he layered some tomato and lettuce.

"What *plausible* explanation do you have for me now?" she asked, eyes riveted by his stacking of the sandwich—Swiss cheese, a real piece of ham, cheddar slice, precooked bacon slices.

"He was trying to get at his sidearm, a noisy flare gun, which he'd foolishly put his coat and sweater over. I guess an unexpected passenger threw him for a loop. He's not usually so forgetful."

Nice. He was trying to shift some of the blame to her. Tammy knew all about that. Her ex-boyfriends thrived on that tactic. "Okay, so Travis was trying to get at his hidden holster. Boris was trying to put the wolves to sleep. What happened after I went to sleep?"

"Not much. Travis fired the flare, which scattered the wolves. A couple of my employees met them to help change the flat, and they finished their route."

"So the truck is here? Load intact?" she asked.

"Of course. We can even go see it if you like."

On the surface, everything added up, and yet the pat answers nagged at her. She'd never heard of anyone carrying around tranquilizing darts. Guns, yes, for protection, but sleeping darts?

"So you still haven't told me why I'm here at your house instead of at a motel?"

"As it turns out, your reservation was accidentally given away. Since there's a lack of accommodations in our town, it not being a real hot tourist spot, and the fact you are here after all to investigate me, I thought what better place for you to keep a close eye on my activities than right here in my home? I've got more than enough room."

In theory, yes. Each room seemed spacious, and yet, his simple presence still managed to overwhelm and crowd her to the point that she felt rather breathless. He slid a plate with a Shaggy-worthy sandwich in front of her.

"You expect me to eat all that?" She eyed the massive offering hungrily. Truth was, she could devour it—and wanted to. But it surprised her that he didn't offer her something smaller and lighter. It's what guys usually did. *Want a salad? Maybe some cottage cheese and fruit?* Most men seemed to assume she was on a diet.

"If you don't want it, I'll have it. I'm always *hungry.*"

The way he said it had her shooting him a glance, but he didn't pay her any mind as he lifted the concoction and bit into it.

Her tummy growled. Screw it. Who cared what he thought of her eating habits? Wrapping her hands around the sandwich, she brought it to her mouth and sank her teeth in. *Mmm…*

She must have hummed her pleasure aloud or something because Reid said, "Good?"

"Better than sex."

Oops. She should have probably kept that one to herself because her simple observation sent the big man into a choking fit.

Chapter Six

Reid was in no danger of choking to death, but it seemed the human didn't know this, as she darted around him and did her best to wrap her arms around his chest and squeeze.

It just made him cough and choke some more, this time in laughter. He wheezed through his mirth, "What are you doing?"

"Saving your life."

"I think I'll live."

Live yes, but allow her to move away, no. When she would have relinquished her hug, he placed his hands upon hers and held them, the skin-to-skin touch just heightening his awareness of her nearness. Something about this city girl drew him. Enticed him and his bear.

As they stood frozen, he could hear the change in her heart rate. It pulsed rapidly and stuttered as he stroked his thumb over the soft skin of her hands. He turned until he could peek down at her. A frown creased her brow, and again, she made to move away, but he caught her with his hands on her waist, for some reason not eager to let her escape.

"What are you doing?" she asked.

I don't know. Instinct not logic currently dictated his actions. But he didn't admit this aloud. "Do you always ask so many questions?"

"Only when I'm trying to understand what's going on."

"Isn't it obvious?"

Confusion clouded her gaze. "No."

Did she not sense the attraction between them? Of course she didn't. She was a simple human. She couldn't know how his bear chuffed at her nearness. How the scent of her aroused him. How he wanted to lay claim to her body.

What the fuck is wrong with me?

Apparently, his grandmother wondered the same thing. "Reid Alexander Carver, what are you doing manhandling our guest?"

Oops, caught harboring naughty thoughts and jolted back to sanity. *What am I doing?*

The city girl jumped, and Reid dropped his hands. Tamara quickly put space between them as she whirled to confront his grandmother. "What is it with people sneaking around here?" she exclaimed.

His grandmother grinned. "We're just light on our feet, child. I see you've recovered from your unfortunate incident."

"Yes, ma'am. Although I hardly call sedating me accidental." She said this with a suspicious glance in his direction.

"Don't ma'am me, child. My name is Ursula, but everyone calls me Ursa, the mother bear."

If only city girl knew how true those words were. Ursa truly was a mother bear, and a matriarch of the clan. Although, he would have added to that title the less official ones of wielder of a mean wooden spoon and champion ear grabber.

"I'm Tammy. I'm with—"

"The insurance company. Yes, Travis told us, and glad we are that you've come. These thefts and tragedies have completely devastated our small community. Poor Reid here has been quite frantic trying to figure out a way to keep the business afloat while things are sorted out."

Frantic? Reid didn't bother to retort at this exaggeration but rather took another bite of his sandwich. If he couldn't feed one appetite, might as well take care of another.

"Yes, well, I'm not here to solve a crime," Tammy stammered. "Merely to judge the company's eligibility to the claim."

"Of course you aren't here to solve the problem. A delicate thing like you shouldn't get involved in violent criminal matters."

It was Tammy's turn to choke on the mouthful of her sandwich.

"Goodness, child, are you all right?" his grandmother asked as she thumped her heartily on the back.

The sound half strangled, Tammy managed to gasp, "Yes, fine. Wrong pipe."

Ha. More like a victim to his grandmother and her straight talk. The city girl might have thought she held an edge when it came to shooting from the hip, but his grandmother wrote the book.

"I see Reid made you a sandwich. Such a good boy. Although I see he forgot a drink." Which his grandmother, in the wink of an eye, had served to their guest, a tall glass of milk. "Once you're done with the sandwich, I've got freshly baked pie for dessert."

"Pie?" Tammy asked faintly before taking another bite.

"Yes, apple pie, with brown sugar and cinnamon. If you like, I can heat it up and put a dollop of ice cream on top. That's how Reid likes his."

Whatever other questions Tammy might have harbored got quelled under his grandmother's steady chatter and feeding. No one went hungry in her house.

To Reid's surprise, Tammy, once over her initial shock, managed to keep up, not just with the food but the barrage of questions. More like an inquisition, one Reid paid way too much attention to.

"How many brothers and sisters do you have?"

"None. Unfortunately." Tammy made a face.

"Why unfortunately?" his ursa inquired.

"Because it leaves my mother too much time to meddle in my life and to Google advice as well as crimes against single women."

"So you are unattached?"

"Oh yes and staying that way," was Tammy's vehement reply as she spooned some of the heated pie dripping in melted vanilla ice cream into her mouth.

Was she humming again? Such a soft sexy sound of pleasure that—

A sharp elbow to his kidney brought his attention back as his grandmother said, "Bad experience?"

"Depends on your definition of bad. My ex-boyfriend was a lying, cheating jerk who thought I should eat a salad at every meal."

Reid couldn't help but retort, "You dumped him because he wanted you to eat like a rabbit?"

"It's not a meal if there isn't protein on the plate."

Reid almost applauded. Too many women nowadays were obsessed with weight, mainly the not gaining of. He appreciated a woman who held a different view and, even better, lived it. The pie plate was clean when Tammy handed it to his grandmother.

"You also said something about cheating?" his ursa inquired as she rinsed off the plate.

"Apparently, he was under the mistaken impression that he didn't have to practice fidelity with me. He thought wrong."

"Reid here doesn't cheat. Although, he does have a temper. Why, one might say he turns into a bear when riled." His grandmother shot him a smirk as she said it.

Tammy, however, didn't catch the pun. Why would she? Humans didn't believe in shapeshifters and the clans saw no reason to change that.

"Nothing wrong with getting mad so long as it's justified," Tammy said.

"Like punching people for supposedly sneaking?" Reid interjected.

"That wasn't out of anger, but self-preservation."

So would throwing her over his shoulder and carrying her up to his room then fall into the realm of self-preservation? Because he was beginning to wonder about his mental state. It sure harbored some interesting visuals about what they should be doing, and didn't include hanging out with his grandmother in a kitchen tearing apart men and discussing the best forms of revenge.

"I should get to my office," he announced.

"Office, but it's dark," Tammy observed.

"Welcome to the north. You just missed the daily dose of daylight."

"What time is it? Last time I checked it was almost suppertime."

"You slept right through the night and the morning. It's actually just after two o'clock in the afternoon."

"Two? You mean I slept practically a whole day?"

He shrugged. "I guess you were tired."

"I was drugged."

"Not that much."

She glared at him.

His grandmother chuckled. "Now, now children. No sense bickering over it. What's done is done. Let's move past that."

That worked for Reid. Especially since instead of riling his temper with her verbal challenge, the city girl roused other things. "I'm going to grab some stuff from my office then head over to my headquarters."

"You work from home?"

"Not usually, although I do have a home office. I should have gone in to work this morning, but I didn't want you to wake alone while my grandmother ran some errands, so I offered to babysit."

"I'm a big girl. You could have left me a note."

"But a note wouldn't have fed you or given you the answers you needed."

"Thank you then, I guess." Grudgingly given, but he preferred that to gushing insincerity.

"Since you're awake now, and Ursa is back, I'll head over to the office. There are some things I need to check on."

She scrambled off the stool. "If you're leaving, I should come with you. You know, to get a look at your base of operations. Maybe talk to some staff."

Did she not understand he was looking for an excuse to escape her, not get closer? The worst part? He couldn't tell her no because she'd probably accuse him of hiding something.

Yeah, a major boner.

Before he could think of a plausible excuse, his grandmother, who for some reason seemed determined to work against him, had Tammy bundled in her ridiculous red parka, wearing a DOT-approved helmet, with her arms around his waist on his snowmobile. He could have taken his truck, but the time it would have taken to warm it up made it not worth it. But next time he should make the effort because having her hugging him, even with their many layers, had a ridiculous effect on him.

One he didn't like at all, but his bear really enjoyed.

Chapter Seven

Tammy wasn't quite sure how she ended up sitting on the ass end of a snowmobile holding onto Reid for dear life as he maneuvered a dark trail.

She blamed the delicious pie and his grandmother, who seemed to have a way of getting her to do and say things she didn't meant to.

I'm here to ask the questions. And yet, Tammy had found herself answering plenty as the old lady drew out most of her life history, a history Reid appeared to listen to even if he didn't add much other the occasional manly grunt and half-hidden smiles.

So much for his claim he didn't have a sense of humor. She'd caught his snort of amusement when she'd told his grandmother how she handled her cheating ex. She'd seen him stifle a grin when she explained her mother's theory about aliens and their radioactive Northern Lights creating mutants. What she didn't understand was the smoldering interest in his gaze as he watched her devour that most delicious sandwich and decadent pie. If she didn't know any better, she'd think he found the sight of her eating arousing.

As if. No man liked to see a woman pack away enough food for two. In her defense, she'd not eaten a decent meal since leaving home.

His possible sexual interest—which probably had to do more with the novelty of someone new than her looks—would have been easier to handle if it wasn't reciprocated. The more time she spent in the man's presence, the more she wanted to eat him, quite literally. Or ride him. Or, heck, have him ride her. At this point, her riled hormones didn't much care so long as they got some action. But Tammy refused to dwell on or travel down that road, for a multitude of reasons.

Firstly, he was under investigation. She didn't get the impression he was the type to steal from his own company and have people killed or taken prisoner, but then again, most mass murderers seemed like the nicest of guys until the bodies turned up in their yard or basement.

Second, a good-looking guy like him probably had his pick of the ladies. She had no interest in having her curvy frame and technique compared against that of another woman. Positive self-esteem only went so far.

And thirdly, she was only here temporarily. Even if he was into big, beautiful women, and they did turn out to be wildly compatible sexual partners, it couldn't go anywhere. It wouldn't last. She had her job and apartment back home. Getting involved wasn't conducive for a healthy emotional heart. She could too easily fall for the big guy and, in the process, end up crushed, and not just by his big ol' body if he collapsed on her after sex.

All the reasons in the world to keep her distance, and yet she snuggled closer as he sped along, the rumble of the engine making conversation impossible. Loud motor or not, though, there was no mistaking the crack of a rifle shot—not to a girl who learned how to fire a gun before she rode a bike. Her dearly departed father had odd notions when it came to father-daughter time.

A second and third loud crack quickly followed.

Before she could wonder if hunting was allowed so close to human habitation, she was tumbling to the ground. A pile of squishy snow broke her fall, but it was the heavy, bulky frame atop hers that made her wonder if she'd die.

Insurance agent investigating a claim suffocated under the body of Reid Carver, who was shot while riding his snowmobile to work. She shoved at his body, relieved when he growled, "Stop squirming, or are you intentionally trying to make yourself and that bright red coat of yours into a target?"

"Someone's shooting at me?"

"You. Me. Both of us. Does it really matter? We're just lucky they missed. No thanks to the giant bulls-eye you're wearing."

"Are you seriously blaming me for this?" she hissed. "Shouldn't the fact I'm wearing a red coat be warning hunters away?" While not quite a safety vest, bright colors were recommended so hunters could differentiate folk from prey.

"If they're hunters."

As his words sank in, her eyes widened, and her voice came out in a hushed whisper. "You're not kidding, are you? You think someone's trying to kill us. But why?"

"Because of your ugly coat? How the fuck should I know?" he grumbled as he lifted his head and scanned the darkness. For what, she couldn't have said. It wasn't as if he could actually see anything, not without those special nighttime vision goggles. But stranger than that, she could swear he sniffed the air.

"I'm going to stand first and see if anyone takes another potshot," he announced.

"Great. Just make sure if you do get hit, that you don't land on me. I'd prefer to not die from broken ribs and internal bleeding."

"Are you implying I'm heavy?"

"Not implying, stating, and I should know given you're squishing me right now."

"To protect you."

Since she didn't have a reply to that, because it was kind of nice, she didn't bother, but she kept a close eye on him as he slowly stood to his full height and did a three-sixty, as if tempting the shooter to try again.

When only silence, broken by whistling wind, was the answer, he reached a hand out to her. Since she'd sunk in some snow, she grasped it and let him heave her out. To his credit, he didn't strain, grunt or exclaim, "Geez, Tammy, lay off the Cheetos."

Given his early words about her coat, she held her breath as she stood alongside him, all too aware of what a vivid target she painted. But the danger seemed to have passed. Or not existed in the first place. Despite his assertion, perhaps he was just paranoid. Maybe the stray shot truly was just a hunter who got too close.

"So now what?" she asked, brushing the snow off her legs.

"Now we go to my office, hopefully without further incident, unless you'd prefer to go back to my place."

If he'd added something along the lines of so "we can warm up", she might have taken the latter option. However, she got more of the impression that he meant he'd drop her off if she was too scared.

She had her dad to thank for her lack of true fear when it came to guns. If someone was going to shoot her, they could do it, whether she was at his business headquarters or his house. If, on the other hand, it was just a stray shot, then she had nothing to fear.

"Let's keep going. I'm here to do a job, not eat your grandma's cooking." Although said cooking would definitely be a perk to this assignment in this sun-forsaken place.

With that decided, Reid ambled over to the snowmobile, which had kept going a short distance after they dove off before halting in a snowbank, where the engine stalled. As Reid tugged at the back end of the machine, lifting and heaving it back a few feet to set it on the trail, she hugged herself, perusing the forest around her.

Did the gunman hide behind the trunk of a tree? Did the sight of a gun track her? And was that a wire strung across the trail?

Tammy might have missed seeing it entirely if not for the speck of snow she spotted that appeared to hover in the air. Except it wasn't levitating. As she approached, the taut wire became easier to identify, but of more concern was its location.

"Fuck me, who the hell did this?" Reid muttered under his breath, apparently having spotted the trap.

"It's right on the snowmobile trail."

"Yup. Chest high and meant to—" Reid paused as if to choose his words. "—um, unseat a driver."

Unseat and injure, Tammy would also wager. The oddest coincidence occurred to her. "I guess it's a good thing someone shot at us."

Reid caught on quickly. "Else we would have run into it. How lucky." Except the grim set to his face didn't seem to really think so at all.

"Was it meant for you?"

"If you're asking how many people know I use this trail, I'd say everybody, just like people in town use it all the time too. There are a couple of trafficked routes. I hope someone's not trying to be a smartass by stringing these up for shits and giggles."

"I don't think it's funny."

"Neither do I, but we have our share of teens and other bored residents who sometimes don't think before they act."

"Do we need to report this?"

"Definitely. And I'm going to suggest they check the other trails. We can't have this kind of stuff happening."

"How do we take it down? I didn't bring any scissors," she joked.

"I've got something. Turn away while I cut it. I wouldn't want the end to snap and hit you."

Tammy gave him her back, and with only the slightest of pings, Reid took care of the wire.

Trail clear, they straddled the snowmobile and got on their way. They made the rest of the trip without getting shot at, which she took as a good sign, and with Reid driving slower than before as he kept an eye out for more wires.

He parked his sled in front of a boring building alongside a dozen or so others. The snowy lot shared space with a lot of SUVs and pickup trucks too, all vehicles capable of handling extreme weather conditions.

Given the biting wind, she didn't pull off the helmet until they got inside, and when she did, a mass of curls tumbled around her shoulders. *I don't even want to imagine how I look.*

"You can put your gear over there." Reid pointed to some hooks and shelves by the front entrance where goggles, helmets, and snow gear hung. She peeled off her layers and slid on the complimentary slippers sitting in a box. Wild hair, rosy cheeks, bulky sweater, two layers of bottoms, big wooly socks, and plaid slip-ons. What a way to make an impression, especially when faced with a perfectly groomed and poised blonde manning the reception desk.

Reid made the introductions. "Jan, this is Ms. Roberts from the insurance bureau. Please give her access to any files she needs regarding the trucks that went missing and their cargo. I'll be in my office if needed."

He's just going to abandon me? Yup. Without a glance in her direction, Reid left, stepping through an open doorway and firmly shutting the door. Hmph. So much for thinking he had the hots for her. Wrong! He couldn't escape her presence fast enough.

"Travis warned me you'd be coming, so I've already got the files ready for you," Jan said as she opened a drawer and pulled forth several folders.

"Have you worked for the company long?"

"Ever since I finished college. I took over from my mom, who was ready to retire. She's spending the winter at some resort place in Florida."

Sunshine and heat? Tammy couldn't help but mutter, "Lucky."

Jan laughed, and like the rest of her, it was a perfect sound. "Our short winter days and cold temps can take some getting used to. But, once you find the right man, you'll see the advantage to cuddling in front of a roaring fire."

Except Tammy didn't plan to stay long enough to hook up with anyone. And she'd ditch the roaring fire. She preferred the less dangerous, artificial kind.

Jan showed her to an empty office belonging to an employee who'd chosen to work from his home office that day.

"If you need anything, let me know. But I imagine these log books will keep you busy for a while." Indeed they would, Tammy thought glumly. She would have preferred listening to perky and perfect Jan instead. The files were exactly as expected, boring reading.

When an hour later she wandered out to find either a gun to shoot herself with or a coffee, Jan must have seen her desperate and silent plea for help because she sent her off with an older fellow for a tour of the facilities. Brief glimpses of the operation for the most part, a peek at the trucks, a few minor conversations with employees. As Tammy went through personal files, she'd set up more in-depth interviews. The one thing she didn't get to see that she kind of expected—and hoped for— was the boss man. Reid proved elusive—or he was avoiding her.

As the workday drew to a close, and dinnertime rolled around, he still had yet to make an appearance. The perfectly efficient Jan was the one who drove Tammy back to the house in her all- wheel drive SUV.

Supper was with Ursula, and what a meal: pan-fried chicken steaks, mashed potatoes, gravy, and biscuits. Enough to make Tammy hum, but it was the chocolate brownies for dessert that made her drool.

Belly full, and shooed from the kitchen when she offered to help clean up, Tammy called it a day and dug out a book she'd brought, but its plot couldn't hold her attention. Boredom sent her to bed early—and alone—as it should be, which didn't explain her disappointment.

Chapter Eight

What a coincidence.

For some reason, the words kept ringing in Reid's head. What were the chances someone would fire at him, and just before he was about to ride into a trap?

How fortuitous. How unlikely. It drove Reid crazy wondering. Was the wire just a prank, albeit a dangerous one? Yes, shifters healed better than humans, and the thick layers they wore outside would have buffered most of the damage, but still, to string a wire across a well-used path? That was more than reckless. It could have proven deadly.

Only the trail Reid used had a report of one, yet that didn't stop Reid from ordering some of his clan out to check the others. He also had them spread the word that if the strung wire and potshots were the antics of bored residents they'd better smarten up or else. Personally, he doubted anyone in his clan was involved in either. He'd stake his life on it.

Which meant a stranger got close enough to do so. *A stranger on my land.* Grrr.

The question of who shot at him—and Tammy—plagued Reid, especially considering his reaction.

When the gunfire cracked, instinct, not one of self-preservation but one of protection, drove Reid. In a mere heartbeat, he'd hit the kill switch on his sled and flattened Tammy on the ground, his body acting as a shield. The bullets fired had come close. Too close.

Rationality dictated they were more than likely stray shots. Possible, but not likely. Who hunted in the dark? A shifter might, but Tammy's coat was too bright for someone to have mistaken them for prey. Add to that the inhabitants of his town preferred to chase down prey on four legs, not two, and he couldn't help but wonder who the target was and why.

A body shot, even from a silver bullet, wouldn't have killed him. Pissed him off, yes. But he would have healed. Tammy, on the other hand…

It chilled him to realize how easily it could have hit her and taken her life. Humanity was so fragile that way.

Unless we changed her, his bear thought to him.

Insanity. For one thing, the risk of change wasn't one to take lightly. It bore risks, deadly risks. Some humans made the transition well, others … yeah, those nobody liked to think or talk about. But the gamble still happened. Their birth rate was too low and their gene pool too small for them not to introduce fresh DNA.

Given that, and despite the deadly consequences to many, they changed humans, but only after careful consideration and if the human was in agreement. Understanding the process seemed to help, as did a strong personality and having a shifter partner with a vested interest in the outcome. Problem was, those in love suffered deeply when the human failed to transform. Another reason why the decision to change was never a light one.

Reid had never sought to turn anyone. Never wanted to. Never intended to. So why the hell was he even thinking about it? How about the even bigger question: why would he even contemplate turning a woman he just met?

Because I'm attracted to her.

More than attracted, he wanted her. Bad.

It irritated him. Reid wasn't the type to covet things he couldn't or shouldn't have. And messing with a human girl who knew nothing of their kind, who was used to city living, and possessed the creamiest skin, didn't make her a candidate. Not for the alpha of a clan.

When he mated, he would do so with a pureblood, what they called those born of a shifter-to-shifter union. This future mate would also probably belong to another clan and their joining would form a bond between two groups. Alliances were what an alpha looked for in a mate, not wild curly hair, or a lack of fear when someone shot at them, or the most delectable lips that, while sexy devouring sweet ice cream, would look so much better if pursed around his—

"Hey, boss, I just woke up and got the message you wanted to see me?" Brody walked into his office without warning, interrupting his train of thought.

Just woke up? Considering it was after seven at night, Reid had to wonder what time his second-in-command went to bed. "I take it you didn't hear?"

"Hear what? Like I said, I got the voicemail and headed right over, although I'm surprised you're still here. I would have thought you'd be at home entertaining the insurance lady."

If by entertain he meant licking her from head to toe before having those plump legs of hers wrap around his waist, then yes, Reid would have preferred an evening at home. But, given he was trying to avoid such a scenario, he'd ignored his guest, left her to her own devices, and arranged for Jan to take her home. His grandmother was more than capable of ensuring she was fed and cared for. Tammy didn't need him.

For some reason the very thought made his bear growl.

Stupid hormones. The winter blues were making him hornier than usual this year. He diverted his mind to the more important matter at hand. "Someone shot at me and the insurance investigator on our way into the office."

"Shot? Are you sure?"

"No. I've gone deaf and imagined the crack of gunfire. Yes, I'm fucking sure. I had some of the boys out this afternoon checking, but as much as it pains me to admit it, you've got one of the best tracking noses around. I want you to come with me and check the trail between here and my house. See if you can find out who fired it. If it turns out the culprit is one of our own, then I want to know it. Everyone should know better than to fire that close to the settlement."

"And if it turns out it's an outsider?"

"Then I want them tracked down and brought to me."

"In one piece I assume?"

"So long as they can talk, I don't care what state you bring them in. Someone's screwing with us, and I, for one, want to know who and why." Forget masking his ominous tone. Reid had every intention of punishing whoever dared threaten him on his own lands.

"On it. But first, I gotta ask, is it true, is this broad the insurance guys sent over cute? Travis says she's got some meat on her bones and quite the rack." Brody held his hands out as if cupping a handful.

A low rumbling growl shook Reid. Not his, but his bear's. It was him, however, who said, "Keep your hands off her." *Mine.*

"Sorry, boss. I didn't know I was poaching."

He couldn't blame Brody for misunderstanding. His words did come across as possessive. *Oh say it like it is. You sound jealous.* And he was. It made no sense. He barely knew the girl and had no interest in pursuing a relationship, but the thought of Brody, or any man for that matter, laying hands on her made him want to crush something. "You're not poaching. I simply don't want any trouble. She's here to do a job, and I don't want anything to fuck with it. We need the claim to go through so we have the funds to replace those trucks and loads. Not to mention, Marie could use some money with the baby close to due." Poor Marie, whose boyfriend, Jonathon, was one of the drivers currently missing. He knew she harbored a hope he still lived. Reid, however, just figured it was a matter of time before his body was found.

"No touching the human. Understood. I'll pass the word along."

And the men in the town better heed it. Reid cracked his knuckles, a sure sign of his agitation. *No denying it. I'm jealous.* Over a city girl he barely knew, but wanted. Good thing Reid wasn't the type of man to give in to his every whim. It was why he'd stayed closeted in his office the entire afternoon. He didn't once go seeking her, not to find out if she had any questions. Not to share his late afternoon snack that his grandmother sent over. He didn't even drive her home. But that was because, when the search party returned and said they'd found tracks but no scent, he wanted to check it out for himself and, with Brody's aid, hopefully spot something the searchers missed.

His bear could use the fresh air and exercise. If he was lucky, he might even find the culprit and work off some excess energy.

Chapter Nine

Tammy couldn't sleep. The comfortable bed wasn't to blame for her tossing and turning. The pillow top cradled her most comfortably. Nor did she shiver with cold, not with her warm flannel jammies and the layer of blankets. Hunger was a word she doubted ever got used in this house. Ursula made sure her belly was full. So why couldn't she sleep?

I know what it is. The house was quiet. Too quiet.

Used to traffic noise, the low hum of cars speeding by, the occasional siren, the hum of her furnace, she found the relative silence broken only by the occasional whistle of the wind outside disturbing.

Yet, there was a time, long ago, when just a little girl, she loved that lack of sound. But back then she had her dad's snores to comfort her, the hunting cabin they owned was an open-plan affair with a bed for her parents and a pullout couch for her. Happy times until the incident.

Maybe some warm milk would relax her—with a shot of whiskey from the liquor cabinet she'd spotted earlier. *But this isn't my house. I can't just go helping myself.* Yet, hadn't Ursula told her to make herself at home, to help herself to whatever she needed? *I could use her grandson, preferably naked.*

Somehow, though, she didn't think the old lady meant for her to debauch Reid when she made the offer, even if he was part of her insomnia problem. Hard to sleep when every time she closed her eyes she imagined a different ending to their tumble in the snow.

It didn't take her long to push the shooting incident to the back of her mind. Shit happened in the woods. Give someone a gun and accidents were bound to occur. Luckily, this one didn't have any consequences. Harder to forget was the weight of Reid, his male instinct to protect her with his own body. To a girl whose last few boyfriends led her to believe chivalry wasn't just dead, but burned to a crisp and never coming back, he was a refreshing change. A man with a gruff attitude, hot body, and, gasp, actual courage.

Now that was hot. Hence the sensual fantasies that wouldn't stop circulating, keeping her awake, yearning, and wanting something she couldn't have.

Sigh. Well, if she couldn't have him, then she could at least drink his milk and partake of a shot of whiskey. Maybe two.

A robe went over her practical and warm flannel pajamas—decorated in a moose wearing earmuffs because she'd not expected to stay in someone's house. Even if she had known, though, she wouldn't have packed something sexier. Tammy was all about the practical. Just look at her coup de grace. To complete her ensemble, fuzzy pink slippers with two floppy ears and cross-stitched eyes covered her feet. A true siren of seduction. Not!

She stepped into the hall, dimly lit by a nightlight, one that somehow magically appeared upon her return to the house. Courtesy of Ursula she had no doubt.

Down the stairs she tread, the silent home strange and yet not frightening. It had too much of a cozy feel for that. So much wood should have made her nervous, especially given what happened to her dad. Yet, despite the definite flammability of the surroundings, her rational side knew it was no more dangerous than her cinderblock-built townhome.

As she hit the main floor, she wondered if Reid was back yet from the office. She'd gone to bed without hearing a thing. Then again, given his ability to move like a silent ninja, he could have tiptoed behind her without her noticing. Yeah, she flicked a glance over her shoulder to check. There was no one there. And, no, the breath she released wasn't filled with disappointment.

Entering the kitchen, she flipped on an overhead light, and it took searching through three cupboards before she located a mug into which she poured some milk before nuking it. She pulled it from the microwave before the timer was done so it wouldn't beep.

Warm cup in hand, she bypassed the opening to the living room and the liquor cabinet to instead wander to the window overlooking the side porch. The light in the kitchen cast a glare, though, making it impossible to see outside unless she pressed her face against the window. Since she didn't want to explain why she left a face print on the window, she flipped off the light and resumed her spot.

It took a few minutes for her eyes to adjust to the darkness, and when they did, she got to admire an alien landscape of snow, the surface marred in spots by snowmobile tracks. A distant light on the garage didn't do much to illuminate the yard, the crescent moon with its wan glow off the snow doing more for visibility. Between the two sources, she had enough light to notice movement coming from the front of the house, a lumbering motion that made its way to the porch steps. Given the proximity, she had no problem recognizing the massive freaking bear that plodded up them. And she meant massive!

Oh my freaking god.

Slowly, holding her breath, she backed away from the window lest the beast spot her and decide a layer of glass wasn't an impediment to a fresh midnight snack. The problem was, backing away meant losing her line of sight on the bear. But she was safe. *I'm in the house. The bear is outside. It can't get to me here.*

Unless it decided to come in.

Her eyes widened and threatened to pop out of her head as she noted the handle to the outside door turning. At that point rationality fled, and she frantically tried to recall what her dad said to do if ever confronted by a bear.

Play dead? She doubted she could fake that, not with fear making her tremble.

Make noise? With what? Somehow shrill screaming didn't seem like the right approach. But what if she found something noisy to bang and scare it off?

The counter behind her was pristine, but above it, on a suspended rack, hung pots and pans. A plan formed. She'd grab two and smash them together in a symphony of noise frightening the bear—who in some Darwinian feat had learned to operate doors—and hopefully bring someone with a gun running.

She managed to only unhook one large frying pan when the door creaked open—and this was just another good reason to always have the habit of locking them, city living or not. A swirling gust of snow blew in.

Shutting her eyes, snowflakes coated her lashes and when she opened them, she couldn't make out much detail-wise about the large shape that loomed in the doorway. Didn't matter. Her father didn't raise a coward, and she wasn't about to become a midnight snack without a fight. She let out a battle cry and swung.

Thwack!

"Ow!"

That didn't sound like a bear. *Oops.*

Tammy backed away as the lights flicked on in the kitchen. She blinked in the sudden glare, and the crystals on her lashes melted leaving her with perfect—and unfortunate—vision. Uh-oh. She blinked some more. Licked her lips. Wet her panties. And not in fear, even if a bear of a man glowered down at her, his irritation over the lump forming on his cheekbone probably the cause.

'Are you seriously accosting me in my home, again?"

"I thought you were a bear," she explained feebly with a wave to the window. "I saw one on the porch, and then something opened the door. I reacted to defend myself."

"With a frying pan?"

She shrugged. "I had to think fast."

"You hit me." He sounded so incredulous.

Welcome to the club. She was becoming well acquainted with the feeling since arriving in Alaska. "Yeah, I did smack you, but I'd say the more pressing point right now is why you're coming in from minus freaking a gazillion outside wearing nothing but the hair on your chest." An impressive chest, mind you, but still, a completely naked one that matched his naked bottom half—*oh my*.

Imagining Reid without clothes was one thing, the reality, another. Her vivid imagination certainly did not do him justice. He was way more impressive in the naked flesh. But why was he bare-assed?

He glanced down at himself as if just now noting his nude state. "I lost my clothes."

"Lost them? How?"

"Well, more like ditched them because they were dirty. Real dirty," he said more loudly before shutting the door and cutting off the stream of cold air swirling around them.

She took a moment to absorb his absurd reply. "Dirty? Really? With what?" What made a man insane enough to strip in this weather? *Did he stain them with blood?* Had she misjudged him after all? Was he a psycho? Her grip on the frying pan tightened.

He noticed, and a single dark brow arched. "Planning to attempt and concuss me again? If you want me flat on my back so bad, you could just ask. But do me a favor, if you plan to ravish me, make sure you use a condom."

"Ravish you? I'm wondering if I should call the cops and have them test you for DNA remains. Exactly how filthy could your clothes supposedly be for you to prefer walking naked in freeze-your-parts-off weather to the house?"

"First off, it's not that cold, which you can see by all my parts being accounted for."

One certain part was definitely not affected by the extreme cold it was subjected to, given how it currently sat at half-mast.

She averted her gaze, but not in time.

A sardonic glint lit his gaze. "My grandmother always did say we had some polar bear in our line."

She ignored his joke. "Where are your clothes?"

"Why?"

"I want to see them."

"You don't believe me."

"It's my job to not believe anyone but to investigate impartially."

"And what do my clothes have to do with your investigation?"

"Establishing your ability to tell the truth."

A smile curved his lips. "This from the woman standing in my kitchen wearing fuzzy bunny slippers, wielding a vicious frying pan because she thought a bear was trying to come in the house."

"I know what I saw." Or thought she had. She really had to wonder if she'd hallucinated it because Reid definitely wasn't acting like a naked man who'd confronted a bear on his porch. Had she imagined it? Or was he trying to divert her from her suspicions? "My nighttime attire and self-defense at least are understandable. You, however, with your nakedness, are not."

"You want proof? Very well. But may I dress before we head back to the garage where I left my stuff?"

"What, is it too cold to walk back?"

"I try to restrict my polar runs to once a day lest certain parts shrivel to the point of no return."

She highly doubted that would happen given its size, but his bare skin was definitely distracting—oh and arousing to the point she wanted to clobber him again just so he'd collapse on the ground and she could give him mouth to mouth to resuscitate him. Wait, that was for drowning victims, not concussion ones. Who cared? He needed clothes so she could concentrate on something other than sex.

Besides, he couldn't very well tamper with anything while dressing, so keeping the frying pan between them, she nodded, and followed him—admiring his bare, flexing cheeks the entire way—as he went to the second floor and entered the door across from her own.

It wasn't long before he emerged in a tracksuit that covered all his bits. How unfortunate.

"Shall we go establish my honesty?" he asked.

She motioned him ahead, wishing she had something more deadly than a frying pan, say like a gun. *As if I could bring myself to shoot him.* But what about the bear she'd seen outside?

"Where did the bear go?" she asked. "You must have seen it as you were coming in. It was on the porch."

"Are you still insisting on that? Do you even hear how that sounds? A bear on the porch." He snorted. "Are you sure you didn't imagine it?"

"The same way I imagined a naked man in the kitchen? No. I know what I saw. There was a bear outside."

"If you say so. Maybe it heard or smelled me coming and took off. The porch does wrap around the house you know."

Again with a plausible explanation that didn't quite ring true. Yet why would he lie? It wasn't as if he stood to gain from hiding the presence of a wild animal from her.

Unless his plan is to lead me outside and feed me to it!

She really needed to stop channeling her mother's paranoia.

In silence she swapped her warm slippers for boots and slid her coat on over her robe. He didn't bother with any outerwear, his only concession to the weather a pair of boots.

He swung the kitchen's side door open and led the way to the garage. The cold bit right though her robe and jammies, and she tucked her hands up her sleeves and her face into the collar of her jacket. Reid, a true Alaskan man, didn't seem bothered as he strode to the garage door. She still clung to the pan in one hand, and her eyes darted nervously from side to side as she followed, seeking in the shadows the beast she'd spotted earlier. They made it without incident, and she stepped into the chilly, but at least bluster-free, space.

Reid walked over to his snowmobile and pointed to the pile of clothes beside it, clothes that reeked of gasoline.

"I told you they were dirty," he said, smirking in triumph. "I sprang a leak in a line and got some fuel on myself as I fixed it. My grandmother would have killed me if I brought these in the house and stank the place up. So, I left them out here for disposal and did a polar streak across the yard."

He's lying. Where that certainty came from, she couldn't have said. But she knew it. Sensed it, even though he had the proof of his words lying on the floor, the same clothes she'd seen him wearing earlier that day. She nudged them with her toes but, other than the reek of volatile fumes, saw no suspicious red or brown stains.

"Satisfied now?"

"I guess."

"My turn then for questions. What were you doing up? Were you spying on me? For that matter, how do I know you are who you say you are? How do I know you're not part of a conspiracy to take down my company, in cahoots with whoever is stealing my trucks?"

Finding herself on the other end of the interrogation and suspicious stick sucked. Tammy sputtered. "Me, a spy? I'm with the insurance company. You can call and check with them."

"I did, and they verified *someone* was coming," he corrected. "But, for all I know, the real Tamara Roberts was killed, and you've taken her place."

"That's absurd."

"No more absurd than thinking I would steal my own trucks and make my employees disappear."

"I have to investigate all the possibilities."

"As do I." For some reason, his words sent a shiver through her, especially since he said them with an intent look.

"You can check me out. I have nothing to hide. I am exactly what you see." A thirty-something, plump, flannel-wearing woman who'd hit an innocent man in the face with a frying pan. Was it any wonder he seemed annoyed with her?

"I know what you show on the outside, yes, but I'm curious about other things."

"Like?" she asked in a bare whisper as he closed the gap between them.

"Such as how you taste."

He didn't give her any more warning than that before his hands spanned her waist and he hoisted her high enough to slant his lips across hers. Any other time, she might have wondered how he hefted her with such ease, but with just a touch, she lost all ability to think. A tingle swept her at the first press of their mouths, an expert embrace where he caressed her lips with his own, explored and teased.

Finally she understood the phrase, 'electrifying kiss'. With every nibble and suck from Reid's mouth, her body sizzled, her blood boiled, and her heart pounded. Her mouth opened at the insistent probe of his tongue, begging for entry and then sinuously twining with her own, drawing a rumble from him, a sexy vibrating sound that caused her to shiver.

So intent was she on the pleasurable sensation his embraced evoke that her whole body loosened, including her grip on the frying pan, which hit the floor with a clang.

Startled, Tammy's eyes opened, and they both paused, lips touching, eyes meeting, her brown gaze caught by his ardent one.

What am I doing?

The spell was broken, and she didn't have to say a word or struggle for him to set her on her feet and step away.

"I think you should go back to bed," he said in a raspy voice.

She simply nodded as she spun on her heel. As if chased by a wild animal—also known as her lust—she raced out of the garage for the house. She didn't check the shadows for bears, but she did glance once over her shoulder before entering the warm haven of the kitchen. Silhouetted in the garage door, Reid stared after her, big and intimidating—and oh so tempting.

The man was dangerous on so many levels. She couldn't help but shudder, not in trepidation. Oh no, she didn't fear Reid, even if logic said she should. Nope, it seemed Tammy still hadn't learned her lesson about men because, damn it all, despite all the reasons to stay away, she desired him.

Chapter Ten

A good thing Reid's beta, Brody, followed him home the previous night. An even better thing Brody had lagged behind as they went to enter the house. The last thing Reid expected was to be met by a pan-wielding human, one who took his nudity as evidence of nefarious deeds.

If she only knew.

At least Brody was a quick thinker. He'd quickly summed up the situation and taken care of the 'evidence'. Reid wasn't sure what to expect when he entered the garage. He knew someone had taken his garments and sled back to the house while he investigated the scene of the shooting. Dousing them with gas proved a stroke of genius on Brody's part.

But poor Tammy. A part of him hated lying, especially since he could see in her eyes she didn't quite believe his fabricated answers. With good reason. Reid had secrets. Lots of them, just not of the type she suspected.

Oh, by the way, I'm a Kodiak bear.

And speaking of suspected, while he'd anticipated enjoying a kiss with the woman, he'd definitely not expected the fire that erupted in every one of his nerve endings. One touch. One taste. He was lost, lost in pleasure and need.

If not for the timely interruption, he would have taken her, right there, in the garage, to hell with the consequences. But of even more concern was the ridiculous urge he had to mark her.

Make her ours.

Even now his bear still insisted on it. It wanted him to march into that house, sling her over a shoulder, throw her on a bed, and strip those ridiculously cute pajamas from her curvy frame. It wanted to lick every inch of her body, bathing her in his scent before chomping on her wrist, leaving a mating scar of a bracelet that would proclaim to all she belonged to him. *Mine.*

Not happening. First off, no one scarred their mate anymore in such a permanent way. In private maybe for fun, yes, however, the clans had long ago moved past the more archaic marking bites to more traditional methods. Still though, something about the city girl brought out the primal beast in him.

He told it to behave. *She is not for me. Or you,* he added when his bear grumbled.

Alphas and clan leaders mated for political reasons, not lust. They ensured a strong bloodline by choosing a strong shifter mate, one capable of bearing natural-born cubs. Not half-breeds. Humans who went through the change and survived could bear their young. However, it took a few generations to breed out the not always recessive human gene and purify the blood.

As if Reid cared about something like that. He could almost hear his bear. They'd long moved past a need for words. Reid just knew what his other half felt, and right now it felt like claiming city girl. *And if someone doesn't like it, they can take it up with my fist.*

If only his life were that simple.

A man in his position was expected to have pure descendants. Not that it was a guarantee his cubs would rule—strength and intelligence usually determined that—but it did make it less likely anyone would rise to challenge.

Thinking of challenge, there was the word he'd tried to avoid since hearing of the attacks but now kept lingering in his mind, and surely in the thoughts of those who'd heard of the incidents plaguing him and his company. Despite no packs or clans coming forth to claim credit, more and more it seemed someone was challenging Reid, spoiling for a fight to take over as leader or to reduce his clan from its position of prominence to one of a much lesser standing.

Never.

He'd not fought and built the company to its level of profitability, not increased the population of his clan, or given them a level of safety and luxury, only to have some upstart think he could waltz in and screw it up, or take over. *Like fuck.*

He would hunt down the bastard responsible, find him, beat him to within an inch of his life, and then make him watch as he destroyed everything his unknown assailant owned. He would make his attacker a poster child for why you never, ever fucked with Reid Carver and those he protected.

And as for the human who disturbed his mental state with her luscious body, strange bravery, and nosy inquiries?

That he'd have to think about, because his only plan—fuck her until she screamed his name and dug her nails into his back—probably wouldn't curb his lust or solve his dilemma. *But it sure would feel good.*

Chapter Eleven

The next morning, Tammy dragged her ass down the stairs knowing she looked like hell. She'd slept only fitfully, bothered by strange dreams of a bear who turned out to be Reid and wolves who weren't wolves at all but men.

I've got to stop watching the SyFy Channel on cable. Apparently her mind wanted to attribute supernatural explanations to mundane events. Crazy and probably due to some weird time zone, oxygen-rich, Alaskan thing. Maybe the lack of fumes from cars was throwing her chemicals off-balance. She knew her hormones were definitely acting up. They'd started from the moment she met Reid and gone into overdrive since their unexpected and ardent embrace. She couldn't help reliving the electrifying moment of the kiss, a kiss that knocked her off-kilter.

A simple embrace shouldn't have the power to make her lust like a schoolgirl with her first crush. Just the recollection shouldn't moisten her underpants over and over. The prospect of seeing Reid shouldn't leave her practically breathless with anticipation then disappointed when she entered the kitchen to discover he'd already gone to work.

Ursula bustled around the kitchen, frying bacon, flipping pancakes, and pouring her juice.

"Can I give you a hand?" Tammy offered.

A snort was her reply. "Child, the day I need help making breakfast for one is the day they bury me. I'm used to feeding gaggles of big men folk. Feeding your little wee self is no problem, so sit your butt down and stop trying to be a good guest. I like cooking, so it's not a bother."

Wee? Tammy practically collapsed in shock. First Reid lifted Tammy as if she were but a feather, and now his grandmother acted as if she weren't some plump goose who wore a size eleven shoe. Her self-esteem could really grow to love the people here. "I don't want to impose."

"You're not. As a matter of fact, it's nice to feel useful." With a grin, Ursula whipped out some utensils, a napkin, and a bottle of syrup—the real maple kind—onto the counter in front of Tammy while at the same time co-ordinating her movements in such a way that she managed to pluck the bacon from a pan and slide perfectly fluffy pancakes on to a plate.

Kitchen poetry in motion.

She let Tammy eat a few heavenly bites before she made her choke. "So what's this I hear about you clobbering my grandson last night?"

Minutes later—after a few hearty whacks on her back by the surprisingly strong old lady and a chug of orange juice—Tammy found her voice. "I, um, thought he was a bear."

Ursula snickered. "He is, especially when he doesn't get a spoonful of brown sugar in his morning coffee. I hear he also managed to give you an eyeful. That boy, even as a child, he could never keep his clothes on."

"It was my fault for not being in bed. I'm sure he never meant to let me see that much of him." A nude image that would stick with her the rest of her life probably. *He should get someone to take pictures or paint him in the buff. He could sell those prints for a fortune.*

And bankrupt poor Tammy's already meager savings because she'd foolishly have to own one.

"Speaking of the rascal, he said to tell you that if you needed to return to his office, to give his receptionist a call and someone would come get you."

Considering the stack of files she'd brought back, Tammy had more than enough to keep her occupied. It would also lessen the temptation to run into Reid and pucker up for a repeat of the previous night's kiss.

Desperate women were not sexy.

I am not desperate. Just horny.

Dull paperwork took care of that. Tammy spent the morning and most of the afternoon poring over truck logs and incident reports. She perused maintenance schedules and the drivers themselves. By all appearances, Reid ran a clean business, a profitable one that, unlike many, included putting his trucks on a strict maintenance schedule that kept them in compliance with safety standards.

He was also extremely efficient about timing loads out from his mines and the local fishery to coincide with supplies coming into the town.

So why this sudden streak of bad luck? If Tammy were given to flights of fancy and conspiracy theories, she'd almost say someone was trying to sabotage him. Which was crazy. That type of thing only happened in books and movies. Real life had its fair share of bad guys, but this was Alaska, and despite the long stretches of untamed land, law and order still prevailed.

But there was bad luck, and then there was not likely. If, let's say, these weren't accidents then who would profit? Given the fragile balance the location of town made getting goods in during the dark and cold months of the year, having one supply run go astray was damaging. Having several in such short order? The town and the company had to be hurting, which was why she wasn't surprised, when she called Jan to ask, to discover that an emergency run was scheduled, a catch-up of sorts.

"When is it leaving?" Tammy asked.

"Either tomorrow or the day after. Usually Reid would have waited until we had a full trailer to pull out, but some of the townsfolk are grumbling about a lack of things they need. Travis and Boris are prepping the truck as we speak."

Tammy hung up, her brow knit in a frown, over what she couldn't have said. Call it a sixth sense, but she had a feeling this trip was a bad idea. Foolish nerves probably on her part, given her scare with the wolves on the way in.

Yet, I arrived alive and well. We all did.

After dinner that evening, with again no Reid—*he is definitely avoiding me*—Ursula, with profuse apologies, went out to meet with her local knitting group. She'd offered to cancel, but Tammy refused.

"Don't change your plans for me. Go. Have fun. I've got plenty to keep me busy," she said with a laugh, pointing at her stack of folders.

"I've left Reid a message to get his big, hairy butt home and keep you company."

"No need. I'll be fine so long as I don't think I see any bears trying to open doors," Tammy said with a laugh.

"Which reminds me…" Ursula scooted off and returned bearing a shotgun and a box of ammo. She handed it to Tammy, who took it with a quizzical look. "Most bears in these parts are benign, so you should refrain from shooting, but just in case you feel in danger, you should have something better than a frying pan."

"What happened to using tranquilizers?" Tammy asked as she cocked open the gun and checked the chambers.

"Nothing like peppering a wild animal with buckshot to get them scurrying, tail tucked," Ursula said with a toothy grin. "Works well with unwanted suitors too. My Tommy, rest his soul, could attest to that."

Despite assuming Ursula exaggerated, Tammy laughed. *Oh, how my dad would have loved her.*

Leaning the shotgun against the wall, Tammy resumed her spot on the couch and tried to concentrate on the files she still needed to read. But her concentration was toast. Alone in the house, she couldn't help an awareness of every single creak, moan, and sigh of the structure. She jumped and twitched, hating her breathless trepidation but, given the events of the past few days, was unable to stem her hypersensitivity. She even checked the doors to make sure they were locked. If Reid came home without a key, then too bad, he could knock for entry. Somehow knowing nothing could get in made her feel better. If that made her a chicken, then cluck, cluck.

Rat-ta-ta.

The brisk rapping at the door, even if half expected, still startled her. Uncurling her legs from under her, Tammy stood and smoothed down her sweater. She'd not changed in to pajamas like she would have at home, opting instead to remain in her yoga pants and comfortable, warm, yet clingy top. She fingered combed her hair as she made her way to the door. She answered the second set of taps, expecting to see Reid. Instead, she confronted a stranger.

So much for city smarts. She'd never have opened the door to her place without checking to see who it was first. Too late now.

"Hello, can I help you?" she asked.

"Is the bear home?" asked a man, his features indistinct within his parka hood pulled low over his brow. Then again, who could blame him with the blustery wind swirling and seeking exposed skin to kiss with its cold embrace?

What was it with the constant references and comparisons to bears around here? "If you mean Reid, then no. Would you like to leave a message?"

"Of a sorts. Come with me."

Tammy, who, with a city girl's instinct, hadn't opened the door all the way, wedged her foot tighter behind it as she said, "Excuse me? I don't know you, and I'm certainly not going anywhere with you."

"You're the insurance girl who wants answers as to what's happening to his trucks and shit?"

The guy obviously knew who she was, but it didn't make her trust him. "Yes, I'm looking for answers."

"Then you'll come with me."

Not likely. Something about the guy rang warning bells. "Who are you?"

"I don't have the time for this yapping shit. You're coming with me and that's that."

He thrust an arm through the door, meaning to grab at her, but Tammy had half expected it. She threw her weight against the portal, wedging and pinching the limb.

He yelled and shoved at the door, his greater weight and strength pushing her back a few inches. Not a good situation. So Tammy did what any girl who'd taken some defense classes would do. She leaned forward and bit his hand. Hard.

In what was a normal reaction, the guy hollered and pulled his injured appendage away from her teeth, and she wasted no time slamming the door shut and locking it.

The guy, though, wasn't perturbed, although she suspected he was deranged as he began to pound on it, demanding, "Open up, you stupid bitch. The boss said to bring your ass to him, and by damn, you're going to come."

Funny how extreme fear could freeze some people but galvanize others. Tammy was an other.

"Screw you," she shouted. "I've got a shotgun that says I'm not going anywhere. Not to mention I'm calling for help. So, if I were you, I'd run fast and far because I don't get the impression Reid's the type to tolerate dickheads accosting his guests."

Given Reid's antics in growing up—which Ursula had regaled her with—she'd wager that Reid would probably vehemently object, with his fists, to anyone acting this way. And, yes, it was perverse, perhaps, but a part of her wouldn't mind seeing it.

"The town's precious alpha isn't here. Not even close. It's just you, me, oh and a couple of my furry friends."

Say what?

The man let out a piercing whistle, but it wasn't the whistle that sent the shiver down her spine. It was the answering ululation of wolves, their eerie howl a horrible timing coincidence considering his words. But she knew better than to think this guy commanded a pack of wolves. Dogs, on the other hand…

Still though, if he thought she was opening the door, he was out of his freaking mind. Rule number one: never leave with your assailant. Which went well with rule number two: don't open the freaking door.

"You'll regret not coming with me quiet like," he yelled as he kicked at the portal.

The solid wood held.

"Unbelievable. It's like living a stupid B movie," she grumbled as she gripped the shotgun and faced the door. Despite his threat, the knob didn't turn—and the deadbolt would have stopped it even if he tried. She didn't hear the sound of breaking glass, and the howling stopped.

She'd almost convinced herself that he was bluffing and had left, when the lights went out.

Chapter Twelve

Just after seven, Jan poked her head into Reid's office. "I'm leaving, boss, and so should you."

"I will as soon as I get done here." And by done, he meant staying late enough to ensure Tammy would be abed—without him.

"Done what? Travis and Boris don't leave until the day after tomorrow. That leaking hydraulic line is going to have to wait until Danny opens his shop in the morning. You've got no paperwork left on your desk, and you've yet to eat a proper meal today."

Because the meal he wanted wasn't on the menu. "I had a large lunch."

"For a supposedly big strong bear, you're an awfully big pussy."

"For an animal lower than me on the food chain, you're treading a thin line between friendship and dinner."

A perfectly groomed blonde brow arched as Jan sassed, "Big tough guy doesn't want to admit the cute little human scares him, so he resorts to threatening his perfect secretary."

"Perfect?" He snorted. "I don't know if I'd go that far."

"Hey, if you can lie about your attraction and avoidance issues with the city girl, then I can pretend I'm in the running for a major raise and employee of the year award."

"I don't know what makes you think I'm attracted to her."

"Let's see. When she was here yesterday, you paired her with the oldest, most solidly married guy on staff to take her on tour."

"Tom is knowledgeable." As well as very dedicated to his wife. Not that the thought crossed his mind when he selected him.

"You called Ursula about six times today to check on her."

Actually it was eight, not that he counted. The stupid call log mocked him the last time he went to dial. "She's a guest in my home."

"And if I told you that Ursula left for her knitting group and the human is alone?"

Alone, wearing those ridiculous pajamas that begged for a big strong bear to shred them from her body? "My house has satellite and hundreds of channels. I'm sure she can find something to keep herself entertained."

"Someone has an answer for everything, so I guess you're not concerned at all then that someone claims they saw wolves out on the eastern ridge."

Jan hadn't even finished her sentence and he was moving. He ignored her laughter as he layered himself against the cold.

"In a hurry, boss?"

Stupid zipper working against him! "Just being cautious."

"Oh please. I just mentioned the lupines as a joke. We get wild ones out there all the time."

"Yes we do, which means no one would suspect a thing if they were part of the gang that accosted Travis and Boris on the road."

Her eyes rounded. "You don't think... Surely, no one is stupid enough to go after a human under your care. The kind of attention that would draw goes over a line even for someone making a bid for supremacy."

"So you also think the attacks are a challenge for power?"

"Seems most likely."

'Who else thinks it is?"

Jan shrugged as she zipped up her own parka, hers co-operating, unlike his that remained jammed halfway, the teeth snagged in fabric. "Pretty much everyone is saying it. Not that we think anything will come of it."

"Meaning?"

"We know you'll take care of it."

Damn straight he would.

Whilst he wanted to believe Jan's assertion no one had the balls to assault someone in his own home, Reid still sped quicker than he should have on the icy roads. Call it bear instinct, but the nagging sensation of something wrong wouldn't leave him. Repeat calls to his house phone kept going straight to voice mail, but that didn't mean anything. With his grandmother out, Tammy probably didn't think she should answer. The smart thing to do to reassure himself would have involved him giving Tammy's cell a call, if he had the number. But he'd not bothered and so now the lack of contact made him grit his teeth–and his bear paced within him, agitated.

The feeling intensified as he pulled into his driveway and noted the lack of lights in the house.

Doesn't mean anything's wrong. Maybe Tammy went to bed. At not even eight o'clock at night? He practically tore the truck door off its hinge when he swung it open, his bear seething as it noted the small wolf tracks crisscrossing the snow of his yard. Those tracks didn't belong to any of his people. Wild wolves had dared invade his territory. Dared to come near his home.

Grrrr. He couldn't help the rumble, not when he knew this was strange behavior considering his home was marked—personally and copiously—in numerous spots. Someone had led the wolves right to his doorstep, and he didn't like it one bit.

He bounded across the icy walk and pounded up the steps to the front porch. He grabbed at the door handle and twisted it, only to find it locked. "What the fuck!"

No one ever locked their doors out here. No one except a city girl, he'd wager.

"Tammy, if you're in there, open this door," he bellowed while pounding. "Ta-m-m-m-y!"

The click of tumblers had barely stopped when he was pushing the door open and scanning the dark interior, not for long as his gaze was caught by the raised barrel of his grandmother's shotgun.

"Are you seriously threatening me with bodily harm again?" he demanded, sniffing the air to assure himself she was uninjured.

"Just making sure I'm not unprepared in case you were entering under duress." For a girl wielding a loaded weapon, she seemed remarkably collected, but beneath her veneer of bravado, he could still sense a thread of fear.

"First off, what makes you think anyone could make me do anything? Two, duress from who? And thirdly, what's up with the lack of lights?"

"Close the door, it's cold out there," she said with a shiver as she lowered the gun.

He slammed it shut then advanced on her. She retreated.

"I'm waiting," he growled. "Answers. Now."

"Short version. Someone knocked. I answered. He demanded I go with him. I said no. He didn't like it. And then a few minutes ago, the lights went out."

"Did he say who he was?"

"Nope. Just claimed he knew why the shipments were disappearing. But that I'd have to go with him if I wanted to find out the answer."

At least she had enough city smarts not to leave with a stranger. "I'm surprised you didn't go with him. Isn't your job to follow all leads?"

She shrugged. "I didn't like the look of him, and I don't do well with orders."

"Well, you'd better learn because I want you to stay in the house while I go check outside to see if he's still around." He also planned to check the electrical line coming into the house. He'd bet his last dollar the outage wasn't due to a downed line.

"Are you sure that's wise? Shouldn't we call the cops or something?"

"To tell them what? That a stranger came to the door and asked you to go with them?"

"A scruffy looking one who tried to force his way in when I said no. Then the power died."

"Happens all the time." It did, usually because of a storm, though, not someone cutting it.

She glared at him. "Why are you making me sound like a paranoid freak?"

"Just pointing out the same things the cops would."

"Fine. You want to confront this guy and the wolves running around outside, be my guest." She strode to the door, swung it open, and gestured to the cold outside.

His brows shot up. "Are you giving me permission?"

"Yes, and would you mind hurrying? We're losing all the heat."

Bemused at the novelty of a human giving him orders, Reid exited his home to investigate. He couldn't help but chuckle as Tammy engaged the locks behind him.

Silly little city girl. Didn't she know a mere door couldn't protect her if he decided to come in?

However he couldn't fault her for taking precautions, she didn't know that her best form of protection had arrived. Even better, judging by the breaking glass he heard around the back of the house, neither did the trespassers.

In seconds his clothes—including one torn winter jacket with a stubborn zipper—littered the snowy ground, and an irritable Kodiak bear went lumbering to find those who dared to threaten what was his.

Chapter Thirteen

The big idiot went back outside. Tammy couldn't believe it, and despite knowing he was out there, possibly with a psycho who enjoyed terrorizing women, she locked the door after him.

If Reid wanted to pull some macho act, then that was his prerogative. However, she wasn't making it easy for anyone to get in. Nor did she offer the shotgun, which in retrospect was a tad selfish. She justified it, though, as her needing it more than him. He was a big guy. He could probably defend himself, and given the wildlife in these parts, chances were Reid carried some kind of weapon—and not just the loaded one in his pants.

I'll bet he's pretty handy with his fists. She could see him as a hands-on kind of guy. An old-school bare knuckles fighter, although who would have the stupidity to engage him she'd have to wonder. While many of the men in town seemed built on larger lines than she was used to, Reid still took the cake when it came to size and sheer menacing presence. Well, menacing maybe to others. Tammy didn't fear him even when he used his big voice or loomed in her space. On the contrary, when he tried to intimidate, it roused her blood and gave her the fire needed to confront him—mostly so she didn't molest him. *What is it about him that makes me want to ravish him when he gets all dominant and growly?*

She didn't underst—

The sound of breaking glass interrupted her train of thought, and the shotgun in her hand rose as she aimed it at the archway leading to the kitchen. At least she assumed she was aiming it there. She had only the faint glow of the outdoors—which was a shade lighter than pitch black—to aid her, as she'd not had time to hunt down candles between the power outage and Reid's arrival.

A swirl of cold air spun through the room, lifting strands of her hair, pimpling her skin despite the sweater she wore. A whole body shiver swept her, yet it wasn't just the low temperature affecting her but the closeness of the howling that erupted. It sounded as if the wolves were just outside.

Where Reid is!

What should she do? He'd told her to remain in the house. Ordered her, as a matter of fact, but one, Tammy didn't obey very well, and two, was she really going to be one of those cowardly girly-girls who cowered inside where it was safe when she had a shotgun and, thanks to her departed father, the ability to hit what she aimed at?

Several yips and growls erupted all at once as if in answer to her silent mental argument. Sharpshooting skills or not, only an idiot would go out there, outnumbered, and in the dark. But, that didn't mean she couldn't do damage from in here via a hole someone had conveniently created.

She crept to the doorway, the broken-glass sound having come from the kitchen. She'd wager the strange fellow had thought to enter the house via the side door by smashing out a pane. If he'd yet to fumble the lock open—*please let him still be outside and not waiting on the other side of the damned arch*—then she could maybe scare him off. He probably didn't expect her to meet him with a gun in hand. And if he wasn't waiting for her, then she'd fire off a few rounds to scatter the furry menaces looking for an evening snack. Thus saving Reid's hide and making him oh so grateful—so grateful he'd have to show his appreciation, naked if she was really lucky.

A great plan, except for one big problem. When she got into the kitchen, there was no human home invader waiting for her. Nope. Even in the dark there was no mistaking the yellow eyes at about waist height as anything but wild. And mean. And probably hungry for a chubby, city-girl snack.

It snarled.

She let out an "eep!" of surprise, and then her training kicked in. She could practically hear her dad and his smooth baritone whisper, *"Breath in. Steady your arm and choose our spot. You'll only get one chance. Don't waste it."*

She had no sooner taken aim than she fired. Even though Tammy expected it, the recoil caused her to stumble a step. Given the confined space, the blast made her ears ring, but despite that, she didn't miss the yelp of pain as pellets hit their mark.

Take that, wolf!

A wolf that didn't move. Nope, despite a muzzle full of buckshot according to the snarl, and the immense shadow still standing in the kitchen, she still faced the beast, only now it glared at her with its one good eye.

"Are you freaking kidding me?" Did it have rabies? Something was surely wrong with the wolf because it should have gone running. *It also shouldn't be standing in the kitchen, seeing as how it can't open doors.*

Obviously someone let it in and had trained it to stand its ground.

"I really hope there are no laws against me keeping your fur, buster, because I am so going to bring it home with me and make some mittens out of it, just for scaring me," she grumbled as she aimed again.

Before she could fire though, a roar—the treble of which vibrated her entire body—split the air. That got the wolf's attention. It got hers too.

What the hell was that?

The wolf swung its head to look behind, and while she didn't see what it did, there was no mistaking the quickness with which it whipped around, tail tucked, and flew out the door.

Anything that could spook off a wolf intent on a tasty, chubby snack probably wasn't something she wanted to meet. That didn't stop her from crossing the kitchen floor under the guise of shutting out the cold.

Such a lie. Curiosity killed the cat, and would possibly claim Tammy's life, but she couldn't *not* glance. She had to see what could cause a grown wolf that had shown extreme signs of aggression, to run off like a cur.

Hand on the doorknob, she froze. Forget closing the back door. Astonishment had her staring as a massive bear, the same one she'd seen previously, she'd swear it, came barreling into view. The wolf, which had not managed to quite escape in time, skidded to a stop on the icy ground, claws digging in.

This was taking the concept of the wild untamed north too far, even for her. Like seriously. A giant wolf and bear facing off in the yard? She really needed to carry around her phone more often, especially around here it seemed, so she could start taking video footage of the increasingly odd shit happening because no one would ever believe her. Heck, she had a hard time believing the craziness herself. *I need a witness.*

Which reminded her… Where the hell was Reid as this all occurred? She would have expected to see him come running at the sound of gunfire. The fact he didn't made her wonder if he was incapable. Perhaps he lay in the snow, injured, dying, in need of her help.

Help she couldn't give while two predators faced off, circling each other with low growls. Could she take the chance they were too occupied with each to notice her sneaking out to look for Reid? Too risky. She needed to scare them off.

Testosterone, even the animal kind, couldn't compete against a gun, or so she surmised as she quickly reloaded the empty chamber with more ammo from her stash in her pocket.

Okay, so when the lights went out, her first thought wasn't to find a candle but to arm herself. She now thanked her gut instinct that catered to paranoia about protection rather than illumination.

With both chambers loaded, she eyed down the barrel, unable to decide which to hit first, a task made harder as the two furry monsters now grappled with each other. Shrugging, she aimed at the snarling mess and fired.

Yelp. The wolf got the first volley—technically his second, making it his unlucky day. With a low howl—that surely meant, *I'll be back to get you, bitch*—he broke off from the tussle and ran. The bear seemed intent on chasing it, but just in case, Tammy decided additional incentive was called for, and given the large target before her—AKA its fat, hairy ass—she fired. And hit!

The bear roared, and it was uncanny how that sound made her think of Reid when she clobbered him with a frying pan. *His grandma was right. He does sound like an ornery bear.*

Before she could go looking for him, because the newest round of gunfire didn't bring him running, another giant wolf came bolting from around the side of the house, its shaggy head turning for a moment to peer at her. Its vivid eyes caught her gaze with an intelligence surely imagined. This second canine beast loped after the injured wolf and bear. Well, after the wolf at any rate. The bear had another idea. It seemed her attempt to send it on its way had backfired.

Uh-oh.

Yeah, it was dark, the sliver of moon barely lighting the yard, but there was no mistaking the way the bear halted in its tracks. Turned. Faced her. Snarled. Stood, and oh yes, began walking in her direction.

"Oh fuck me to hell and back," Tammy cursed as she reeled back into the false safety of the house. Her fingers fumbled for the ammo in her pockets, the simple act of reloading betrayed by the shaking of her hands.

It didn't help that the upright bear roared. Not a happy roar. As if such a thing existed.

Where was a picnic basket or a park ranger when you needed one?

"Shit. Shit. Shit." She took her eyes off the monster for a minute and peeked down at the gun. She managed to jam the shots into the empty chambers, clicked the gun shut, and lifted it to aim, but she didn't fire.

Her jaw dropped, and she might have stopped breathing, as she stared upon not a bear, but a very naked Reid, who, sounding like a very pissed-off bear, said, "Don't you dare fucking shoot."

Chapter Fourteen

Since the day Tammy, the chubby city girl, dropped into Reid's arms, she'd done nothing but wreak havoc on his life, body and emotions. She'd also shot him. In the ASS! With silver buckshot no less, and it fucking stung.

So was it any wonder when Reid noticed his beta—who in his wolf shape could run much faster with his unblemished buttocks—streaked past him that Reid turned around to confront the bane of his existence. The siren of his dreams. The woman who dared to reload her gun and aim to shoot again.

Beyond thinking or caring, Reid did something rash, something he would have punished anyone in his clan for. Something so unlike him. He changed, not quite before her eyes, seeing as how she foolishly took her gaze off him for a second to reload her damnable weapon. But close enough, so that when she snapped the gun closed and aimed, she faced a very irate, naked male.

"Reid?"

He could see the confusion in her gaze, hear it in her tone. But he was past rational thought, especially with his butt burning something fierce as the silver reacted with his shifter flesh.

"Why is it every time I turn around you're trying to either hit me or shoot me?" he bellowed.

She should have cowered before his rage. Even Jan, his rascally receptionist, or Brody, his outspoken second-in-command, knew better than to provoke him once he snapped. Apparently, nobody thought to warn Tammy.

Spine straight, eyes flashing, and cheeks hot with color, she spat, "Maybe if you didn't sneak up all the time, I wouldn't have to hurt you. Speaking of which, where the hell is the bear this time, and don't tell me you didn't see him, Reid Carver? He was right there. And where the fuck are your clothes? That's what I'd like to know. Do you know how disturbing it is to have a fight with a man who's naked?"

"Not as disturbing as getting shot in the ass, I'm sure," he retorted, twisting his hips to show her his offended posterior.

"How is that my fault?"

"You shot me."

"I shot a bear."

"Yup."

And still she didn't make the connection. Denial. Some people had it stronger than others.

"Just because you're big and mean, and awfully hairy in some places, doesn't make you a bear."

"Oh yes it does." Yeah, he told the truth. Yeah, it was against his own rules. He didn't fucking care. *I make the rules.*

"Hate to break it to you, but no, you're not. Big and hairy, yes, but you're as human as I am."

"No, I'm not human like you. I'm a shapeshifter. A Kodiak bear to be precise."

She snorted. "Seriously? You did not just claim that. I might be a city girl, but I'm not gullible."

"Then explain how you shot a bear in the ass, but I'm the one with the wounds." He pointed to his posterior. Impossible as it seemed, she looked even cuter when she blushed.

"I don't know how you got shot. But I know what I was aiming at, and it wasn't human."

"Exactly."

"Oh my freaking god, you actually believe that. You think you're a bloody bear."

Her mocking tone was what did it. Reid had never morphed so fast in his life. Nor had he ever heard such a piercing shriek.

"Ohmyfuckinggodyou'reafuckingbear."

Well duh. About time she believed me.

Believed and was about to take protective measures. Up came the gun, but before she could fire, he lunged forward and batted it to the side. She squeaked and backed away from him, fear finally making her tremble. But he didn't want her afraid. He just wanted her to believe him. *And to stop fucking shooting at me.*

Given he'd just changed shapes twice in quick succession, he couldn't manage a third, not for a few minutes at least, maybe longer. However, how was he to reassure Tammy he wouldn't hurt her, even if she was driving him crazy?

Maybe if I looked harmless? Although how an enormous Kodiak bear was supposed to look benign, he didn't know. He could start maybe by not looming over her. He sat down, let out a yelp as his wounded butt hit the floor, and stood up again.

Tammy took that moment to dive for the kitchen island and rearmed herself with, yup, the same damned frying pan as before.

Frightened or not, Tammy didn't back down. Her wild eyes and tone still held a hint of her indomitable spirit as she brandished the frying pan with a threatened, "Come near me, and I'll hit you."

If he could have, he would have sighed, or maybe laughed. *Does she honestly think she can stop me with a frying pan?* Given his vocal cords couldn't handle normal human sounds, he had to settle for an exhalation of breath.

She took that as a sign of impending violence and waggled her cooking ware at him with a stern, "Stay back, or I'll bash your brains in."

More like give him a headache. Since the worst she could do was give him a bump on his noggin, he ignored her for a moment so he could swivel his head and peer at the damage she'd wrought.

My poor ass. While he would heal quickly from his wounds, he still needed to get the silver shot out first. Given its location, he'd need help.

Where is my grandmother when I need her?

He guessed he'd have to wait until she came home and tended him.

At the triumphant howl of his beta, his ears perked. Sounded like someone was enjoying a more successful evening than him. Reid just hoped Brody had captured the challenging wolf for questioning. Something about the odd attack on his home made no sense.

The wiliness of the truck and trailer disappearances didn't match up with the sloppiness of this home invasion. Not to mention the stupidity. Reid couldn't wait to get his paws on the wolf and—

Tammy interrupted his train of thought. "Hey, Reid, or should I call you Baloo?"

She did not just call him that. He rumbled a warning.

"Baloo it is. So now that you've proven you're a freak of nature, do you mind changing back? While I'm adjusting to the idea you might not eat me, I'm not comfortable with the fact I'm in a kitchen with a big-ass, freaking bear."

He growled.

"Sorry if the truth offends you, but really, you gotta admit, your ass is pretty damned big."

Why me? He was beginning to think he preferred her in hysterics over mocking. Where was the respect? The obedience?

Apparently, behind her mighty frying pan shield his city girl felt invincible, or so he surmised, as she tread carefully from the side of the island, gave him a wide berth, and headed for the back door. "If you don't mind, not all of us have a giant fur coat and a layer of fat to keep us warm."

Fat? Did she seriously call him fat? He bared his teeth. She ignored him as she swept past and shut the door, locking it for good measure, which, given the broken pane, was oxymoronic. A conclusion she came to as well.

"Got any duct tape?" she asked, a moment before the kitchen flooded with brilliance. Someone had restored the power. He blinked at the sudden glare.

She gasped. "Baloo, you're bleeding."

Well duh. You shot me. Of course, she didn't hear that, but she must have caught something of it in his expression because she bit her lip. "I guess saying I'm sorry might not cut it this time. Can I take you to a hospital? Or a vet?"

He shook his head.

"At least let me wipe off the blood."

With less fear, and her pan hanging down by her side, Tammy marched back to the other side of the island and, miracle of all miracles, laid down her weapon. As she ran the water, she ducked out of sight, scrounging in the cupboards.

He took that opportunity to switch shapes, the process taking longer than usual and more painful. He groaned as he found himself on human hands and knees on the floor.

"What the— Hey, you're back. Not that you were gone. But I see you're just a naked man again."

"Just?"

"Sorry, a hairy naked man with holes in his ass."

"I'm glad you find this entertaining. Meanwhile you're not the one bleeding on the floor."

"I said I was sorry, and look, I got you a warm cloth for the blood." She held up a dripping washcloth.

"Great. That just makes it all better."

"Don't get snippy with me. I was just protecting myself."

"Funny, because I was also protecting you, but that didn't save me from injury."

"Are you the type of guy who whines and harps and can't accept an apology?"

"I'll accept your apology once you fix this mess."

"Fix it how?"

"Grab the first aid kit, don't forget the tweezers."

"Why do I need tweezers?"

"You shot the silver into my ass. Now you can take it out." He couldn't stop a slow smile from curling his lips.

Did he enjoy her dropped jaw and incredulously wide eyes? Yes, he most certainly did. What he didn't trust though was how those quickly disappeared, replaced by a smirk and a gaze dancing with mirth. "You want me to play nurse, Baloo? Fine. Go lie on the couch. Exactly where is this first aid kit with the stuff I need?"

"Cabinet over the fridge." While she fetched the kit, Reid hit the laundry room off the kitchen and grabbed a few clean towels. No sense in riling his grandmother by streaking the couch in blood. She'd probably have as much sympathy for him as Tammy did and would make him scrub it clean if he stained it.

Damnable women. And to think he'd harbored lusty thoughts about the human. Well, he wouldn't have to worry about that anymore. He was cured. Over her. Not interested.

A lie that lasted all of thirty seconds.

Squashed under her frame as Tammy straddled his thighs and sat down on him, he couldn't help a spurt of pleasure at the closeness. Not that he showed it. His erection was hidden out of sight in the sofa cushions. He craned to glare at her over his shoulder.

"What are you doing?"

"Getting into a comfy position. It's bad enough you've got me plucking shot out of your cheeks. I'm not wrecking my back hunching over you."

"Your bedside manner sucks."

"How would you know? We've never gone to bed," she teased.

He would have retorted but clenched his teeth instead as she yanked the first piece out.

"So, how long have you been a bear?" she asked in a conversational tone as she worked on him.

"Since birth."

She paused. "You were born like this?"

'Yes, but we don't actually turn into our animal until we hit about five or six. If at all. Something about our hormones changes around then and makes the shift possible."

"Fascinating," she murmured. "You said we. So you're not the only one who can do this."

Damn. She'd caught his ill choice of words. "No, there are others. But not many," he hastened to add.

"All born that way?"

"Yes." More or less. But no need to give away all his secrets.

She kept plucking and wiping with her warm cloth, her touch softer than he would have expected, gentle. It soothed his bear, and despite the scenario and his earlier assertion that he wanted nothing to do with her, he couldn't help the arousal burning through him. He blamed that on the adrenaline from the fight. What man, or beast, didn't enjoy a good fuck after battle? It had nothing to do with city girl's soft hands or enticing scent.

"Is it something in the water?" she asked after a few minutes of silence.

Hunh? "What on earth are you talking about?"

"Well, if you're born that way, and it's only happening here, then it's obviously something environmental. Oh my god. Don't tell me my mother was right. It's those Northern Lights, isn't it?"

Laughter erupted from him; he couldn't help it.

"Hey, it's not that funny."

"Yes it is. First off, who says shifters are only confined to my town?"

"You mean there are more of you, *out there*?"

"Around the world, city girl. Heck, your neighbor could be one, and you'd never know."

"Impossible."

"Why impossible?"

"How can you hide something like that?"

"Easy. Don't show humans." A rule he'd just broken. Good news, though, she was taking it remarkably well now that the initial shock had worn off.

"Doesn't it show up on like blood tests and stuff though?"

"First off, we try to stay away from human doctors, and secondly, no, our blood shows up normal. DNA sequencing, however, that's a whole other story. But we avoid those types of tests."

"That's crazy."

"No more crazy than you thinking you could take me on with a frying pan."

"Admit it, you were shaking inside."

"With laughter."

"I thought you didn't laugh," she pointed out.

"I don't." Or he didn't much until his city girl came along. Then again, he'd not found much to laugh about since he took over leadership of the town and the responsibilities that came with it.

"So now that I know your deep, dark secret, are you going to kill me?"

"What?" He craned to peek at her over his shoulder and found her staring back with a serious mien.

"Obviously, you guys, shifters or whatever you call yourselves, are good at keeping this a secret. So either that means you've got some spell or potion to shut me up, or you're going to kill me."

"You could also just promise to not tell anyone." *I could also keep you here. Mine. Forever.* His bear liked that last idea.

"You'd trust me, an almost stranger, with a secret like that?"

Funny how she was the one to point that out. It was the argument he would have used had anyone else in his clan done the same foolish thing. "Are you trying to convince me I shouldn't trust you?"

In the process of applying a clean bandage to his now silver-free cheeks, she paused. "Of course not. It's just I know how hard it can be to trust someone. You think their word is good. That they mean what they say, only to later find out they're liars who would betray you in a heartbeat."

He understood in that moment that she didn't refer to this situation but her past, a past with others who'd obviously made her wary of believing in people.

"What do you suggest we do? You're right. Maybe I should take you at face value. I mean, let's look at the facts, everything you've done since I met you has involved some kind of injury to my person. Obviously, you're a threat to me."

"Me?" The way she squeaked roused the predator in him—among other things.

When she went to escape, her feet hitting the floor poised for flight, he rolled onto his side and caught her, one arm whipping around her thighs, trapping her. With his fingers tugging at her waist, he forced her to kneel beside the couch, close enough that his other hand could curl around her nape and drag her close. Close enough to whisper against her lips.

"And just where do you think you're going, city girl?" Because didn't she understand she'd roused the lusty beast? There was nowhere she could run that he wouldn't find her. *Because she's mine.*

Chapter Fifteen

Where am I going? There was a question with a few answers. Away was probably the most sane one. Crazy was probably the most apt. But going nowhere ended up the action of choice once Reid slanted his mouth over Tammy's.

As before, instant fire ignited her blood. He touched her, and she melted. Forget the fact she'd just spent the last little while plucking pellets from his rock-hard ass. Who cared if he turned into a massive, shaggy bear? Or that someone had tried to kidnap her?

Reid kissed her, claimed her lips, and she couldn't think past the instant web of pleasure his touch aroused. And she meant aroused.

One of his hands cupped her head while the other slid under the hem of her shirt, his large hand palming the skin of her back, an electrifying skin-to-skin touch. Her own hands strayed to the bare skin of his chest, stroking the bulging muscles of his shoulders, skimming his pecs and the fuzz covering them. She felt the thud of his heart, the heat of his flesh, the warmth of his breath. All of it combined to create a mesmerizing spell of seduction.

Somehow she found herself lying alongside him on the couch, a sliver of it only given his size, but she didn't fear falling, not with him holding her. They were pressed tight together as their lips embraced and tongues dueled. One breath, one desire, one step away from—

"Reid Montgomery Carver, unhand our guest right this instant and get some clothes on. This is not appropriate behavior for a man in your position."

The shocked—and yet amused—voice of his grandmother acted as a cold bucket of water on their make-out session.

Oh my god. Mortified, Tammy struggled to escape Reid's embrace, but he wouldn't let her go. On the contrary, his grip tightened.

"I was liking my position perfectly fine until you interrupted."

"And a good thing I did. Did you know we have *wolves* outside?"

The inflection might have fooled Tammy before, but with her wits returning, she quickly clued in that his grandmother implied something more.

"I know about our furry visitors. They're being taken care of by Brody."

"You actually let someone else do something for a change?" His grandmother seemed shocked.

"I was injured, and Tammy here was kind enough to help me."

His grandmother's tone changed as concern threaded it. "Injured how? Did the wolves hurt you? Do you require medical attention?"

"Give me a little bit of credit. As if those mongrels could harm me. No, I owe the holes in my ass to none other than our guest." Tammy groaned as she buried her face in his shoulder. Reid chuckled. "Apparently someone loaned her a shotgun, and city girl here used it."

"On you?"

"In her defense, Tammy thought she was protecting herself from a bear at a time. She's since learned about my special situation and has done her best to patch me up and kiss me better. Which, I'll admit, was working quite well until someone interrupted."

Yup, Tammy was going to die of embarrassment any minute now. How she wanted to slink off and hide, but Reid wouldn't let go. Even as he shifted to seat himself, he dragged her with him, probably as a shield for the erection still poking at her.

Cheeks hot, Tammy kept her gaze trained on the floor, unable to meet that of his grandmother who surely thought she was a violent hussy.

"So she knows?"

She felt more than saw Reid's nod.

"Oh dear. What have you done?" Ursula didn't sound pleased with the turn of events at all.

Tammy hastened to reassure her. "I've already promised to not say a word."

"I'm sure you won't because it would be a shame if you did. I'd hate to have to dig out grandma's recipe. Fresh basil is so hard to find this time of the year."

"What recipe?" Tammy squeaked.

"Never you mind. I'm sure we won't have to resort to that, will we?"

Tammy's brown gaze met the stern one of Reid's grandmother. Gone was the friendly matron.

Hello, predator. How had she not noticed before what big teeth Ursula had? *All the better to … gulp … eat me with.*

"Stop trying to scare her," Reid growled. "And find me some pants. Now that I'm patched up, I should go see what Brody's caught."

Tammy was only too glad to escape when his arms finally released her, but she couldn't help hearing the echo of his ominous words as she fled up the stairs.

"I'm not done with you yet, city girl."

She couldn't decide if she liked the sound of that or not.

Chapter Sixteen

Despite knowing he needed to locate Brody and have him report, a part of Reid wasn't eager to leave Tammy. His bear didn't want him to go at all. The attack on not just his home, but the attempt to kidnap her, had set off a protective instinct within him that went beyond what he usually felt when his clan or someone close to him was threatened.

Reid didn't know his city girl well enough to have developed feelings, but his man side had no problem recognizing that his wilder side, his beast in other words, worked on a different wavelength.

His bear had taken a shine to Tammy. Instinct, scent, something intangible to the human but oh so clear to his bestial half, drew him to her. Reid wanted to fight it. Tried. But, so far, he was failing miserably.

Did he curse and regret his grandmother's untimely intervention? Yes and no. Yes, because he'd been so close to tasting nirvana. But, at the same time, he thanked her arrival because he was neglecting his duty as alpha to his clan by not pursing the threat to him and his people.

Hurriedly dressing, Reid managed to escape more haranguing from his grandmother who was in the kitchen feeding Travis. Brody had sent him into the house as an added layer of safety. Given the shit of the past few days, Reid would probably have him stick around. Young and hot-headed didn't mean he wasn't a good fighter, and Reid knew he could trust him to protect not just his ursa but Tammy and anyone else in danger.

As Reid slipped outside, he took a moment to survey the surroundings. Angling his head, he sniffed. Even in the crisp, cool weather, the stench of wild wolf filled the air. With the outdoor lights working and his sharp eyesight, it wasn't hard to note all the tracks marring the snow in and around his home. Most belonged to him and his close family or acquaintances, but overlaying them were paw prints. Wolf ones to be exact. Most of them were small, which indicated they belonged to the regular variety of wolf. However, as he circled around the house, only a few steps past his electrical box, which hung open and showed signs of electrical tape from a temporary fix, he found the human footsteps sitting alongside a pile of clothes.

He crouched down and brought his face close to them. Growled. The stench of wolf, a shifter not belonging to his clan and yet somehow familiar, clung heavily to the fabric. The same scent as that of the canine he'd engaged fleeing from his home. *Because my brave and stupid city girl shot him full of silver.*

He didn't know if he should throttle or kiss her. Maybe both.

Inhaling deeper, he attempted to sort the scents, seeking another marker, any kind of indicator as to who might have sent the man on what Reid suspected was a suicide mission. And that's what it was. A foolhardy attempt to strike at him that would have failed. Oh, perhaps the stranger might have managed to kidnap Tammy, but no way would he have gotten far. With a band of wolves leaving a scent trail anyone could follow, Reid and his clan would have tracked him.

As Reid shook out the garments, searching for a clue as to the guy's identity, footsteps crunched in the snow. He peeked up at his beta.

"You caught him?"

Brody nodded. "Oh yeah. Your guest has quite the aim. Even you and your slow bear legs would have managed to catch him."

"I had other things to take care of."

"Something more important than a rogue wolf poaching on your territory?"

Yeah, a feisty city girl who thought she could take me down with a frying pan. "I was making sure the insurance girl was okay."

"Sure you were. I think it's more because someone had an ass shot full of silver. Getting soft in your old age?"

"You're not funny."

"Says you." Brody grinned. "So did she kiss it all better?"

"She plucked it out, yes."

"Before or after you made out?"

"We're not involved."

"Dude. Don't lie to me. I can smell her on you."

Some secrets couldn't hope to remain hidden. "Ursa walked in just before we got to the good part."

"Still cock blocking, is she?"

Cock blocking and reminding Reid that he was destined for things other than a tempting city girl with wild curly hair. "Forget my grandmother and her need to interrupt my sex life. What have you learned from our uninvited guest?"

"Not much. Unless you count whining. Apparently he seems to think we should treat him nicer because he's one of us. As a matter of fact, he's one of the missing drivers. The one we recently hired."

"He's not dead?" Not only that, but obviously in cahoots with whomever targeted Reid and his company. "Is he fucking stupid? What kind of idiot returns to the town he screwed over?"

"A none-too-bright one, who, like I said was whining we should treat him nicer."

"Oh really? Doesn't like our hospitality? I think it's time I met him and showed him just how much more hospitable I can be." Reid and Brody headed to the garage. "So how come you ended up at my house anyway? I thought you were home packing and organizing the clan enforcers so you could head out with the next truck shipment."

"I was, but when I heard there were wolves sniffing around, I called some of the boys and headed out for a peek."

"Without contacting me?"

"I tried, but your phone wasn't answering."

Probably because Reid had left it on his desk when he did his mad dash from the office.

"Fair enough, but that doesn't explain why you came to my home."

Brody rolled his shoulders. "Intuition. Given the potshots taken at you and the insurance broad the other day, I figured it might be prudent to check in here first and then sweep outward. Of course, when I arrived, you were already romping in the snow, at least until your wide ass got shot."

"My ass is not wide." And why did people keep implying it was. He was a bear. A Kodiak. Everything about him was big.

"Says the guy who couldn't chase down a mangy wolf."

"Anytime you want to arm wrestle, let me know."

Brody shook his head and held his hands up in surrender. "No thanks. We both know I might be fast, but when it comes to brute strength, I am not a bear."

Manliness reasserted, Reid asked, "I take it Boris was the one to hook the power back up." The moose was the only guy Brody would have grabbed for a perimeter check who would have had the know-how to splice a broken line. Reid sometimes wondered if there was anything the big moose didn't know how to do. Other than smile. Boris had an acerbic wit, but since his return from his tour overseas, he rarely cracked a grin.

"Yeah. Boris is the one watching the wolf. More like glaring at him while he sharpens his knife." Brody chuckled. "I swear, the sound that blade makes running along that stone... Fucking spooky. If that wolf's not begging to talk by the time we arrive, I'll be surprised."

Boris might not speak much, but he had the art of intimidation down to a science.

"I noticed Travis was in the house, I assume to keep an eye on the women. Who else we got out here?"

"A few of the younger hotheads are chasing down stray wolves and keeping an eye open for anything that doesn't belong. They already found the guy's sled, but it's clean. No plates, filed serial numbers. Nothing to give us a clue."

"Do you think there are more like him out there?" Reid asked.

Again, Brody shrugged. "Hard to tell. I mean everything about this attack is odd. I mean one guy and a pack of wild wolves? He had to know it wouldn't succeed."

Yet it almost had. If he'd not arrived when he had, would Tammy right now be in the hands of the enemy? Or staring sightlessly at the sky?

Remembering the threat to her stirred the simmering rage within him, just in time too because what he had to do next couldn't be done while in a soft frame of mind.

When Reid entered the garage, Brody at his heels, he was just in time to see Boris run his thumb along the edge of his blade. The coppery scent of blood filled the air. The acrid stench of fear didn't.

Despite his position—tied to a chair, bleeding and surrounded by three very unhappy predators—the wolf they'd caught exuded cockiness. Hell, even with one eye gummed shut, he managed a smirk.

Reid racked his brain for a name. He'd only met the guy once after they hired him. He didn't recall much other than he'd feigned submission well, keeping his eyes downcast the entire time.

Snagging a stool by his workbench, Reid banged it off the floor as he set it down before the canine. Still no reaction. Either the wolf had balls of steel, was stupider than he looked, or something was afoot. *Should I be calling in reinforcements?*

Was this just the precursor to an all-out war? Were enemy shifters even now preparing to descend upon them?

Reid bitch slapped the doubts. No way. While he and those guarding his clan might have missed a few wild wolves and one of their kind sneaking into their territory, anything on a larger scale would have sent out alarms.

He didn't waste time with niceties. "Who are you working for?"

No answer.

Reid gave Boris a nod. The moose didn't ask questions or hesitate. The mutt didn't need a pinkie finger to survive, but he did need to answer Reid if he wanted any hope of dying clean.

"That was just a warning," Reid said in a cold tone after Robert, the driver who should have stayed dead, stopped screaming. You would have thought he would be grateful they immediately cauterized the amputated spot with the flame from a blowtorch. Some people would have let him bleed to death. But Boris had learned his craft while serving overseas. Not from the US army, but as a prisoner. He didn't talk about it much. None of the men who'd returned from that camp did. But some things a man never forgot.

Spit flew as the stranger yelled, "Crazy bastard. I'll have your balls for this."

Reid arched a brow. "You will? How? In case you hadn't noticed, I hold all the cards here, mutt. You'd do best to answer me."

The wolf clamped his lips tight.

Reid inclined his head, and Boris stopped wiping his knife. Before he could apply the freshly cleaned blade to a new finger, Robert, his eyes rolling with fear and pain, yelled, "Leave my fucking fingers alone, you psycho."

"My good friend Boris here will stop removing body parts when you answer my questions. Who is your leader? Who are you working for?"

"What makes you think I'm not here for myself? Maybe I'm the one making a run at your position. Everyone in these parts knows you're weak."

Incredulity made him snort. "Weak? Excuse me, what rock have you hidden under that you would think that?"

"Everyone knows you had the clan handed to you on a platter when your daddy died. Never had to work for it, or fight for it. It's not the shifter way. Only the strong should govern."

"Says someone with little to no brains. It takes more than the strength of a fist to rule." It was one of the few things he remembered his father saying. That and never show mercy to those who would hurt the pack to benefit themselves.

And as for no challengers to the spot, Reid had offered to fight when the alpha position became available through tragedy. It wasn't his fault no one took him up on it. Of course, back then, he'd just gotten home from serving his time in the war. If people thought him intimidating now, they should have met him then.

"Those are the words of a coward." Robert spat on the floor. "Look at you. Sitting there all high and mighty. Easy to be a brave man when you've got a posse at your back to help you beat on a man tied up. Let me loose if you're so damned confident."

Did the wolf think they kept him tethered so he wouldn't run? Foolish mutt. The restraints were to keep him from thrashing as they removed body parts in exchange for answers. Reid leaned forward. "Ironic words seeing as how when I came across you, you were terrorizing a human woman. And look who's disparaging my alpha status. You're so alpha, you can't even muster a true pack, only wild dogs who don't know any better."

"They know enough to obey, and they're expendable. As for the human girl… Can you blame me for going after her? She looked yummy." The male lewdly licked his lips.

A well-placed fist knocked the wolf in the face and sent him and the chair he was tied to crashing to the floor.

Seething with rage, Reid could barely restrain the bear within. *Don't you threaten what's mine!* Where the possessive thought came from he couldn't have said, but no matter the origin, he reacted to the mutt's words.

The canine laughed. "Ooh, someone has a soft spot for a *human*." A sneer twisted his bloody lips. "Good to know. Wait until *he* finds out."

"He?" Reid leaned down and grabbed the man, chair and all, lifting him from the floor in one powerful fist, dangling him at eye level to growl, "Who is this *he* you're referring to?"

"Just the man who's going to bring you down."

"So you admit to not being the one in charge?"

"Nope. I'm just a soldier. One who gets to have fun."

"Fun? You call taking potshots and terrorizing women fun?"

"Among other things. I hear someone's been having a problem with deliveries lately." Robert smirked.

"What did you do with my truck?"

"Don't you mean trucks? The one I was driving was easy. Steven's too. You never even suspected."

"You mean none of you were actually attacked? It was all a sham?"

"Not all. That idiot Jonathon, the one with the prego girlfriend, should have taken the money offered him. But, no, he turned us down out of some misplaced loyalty to the clan. Weakling. That's what happens when you put down roots. You get soft. He put up a good fight when we came for him. But we had numbers."

"So you're not working alone?"

"*He* has many of us working for him."

"To what purpose?"

The sharp crack of shattering glass delayed an answer, an answer that would never be forthcoming as the wolf Reid held went slack-jawed and sightless, the exit hole of the bullet oozing blood from the center of his forehead.

Heck, it barely missed killing Reid, grazing as it did past his head, nicking his ear in the process.

"Damn." Reid flung the dead man to the side, then he, Boris, and Brody hit the floor, in expectation of a hail of bullets.

Silence and minutes trickled past. Reid glanced over at Boris and pointed to the door. To Brody, he signaled the unbroken window while he made the shattered one his objective. Crawling like a snake, which his bear snuffed about it, not liking the comparison, he made his way to the opening, which sat about waist high on him. Cold air flowed through, along with the noise he would expect. Wind whistling, branches rattling. Nothing else but…

"Hey, you guys all right out here?"

Nothing but Travis wandering out from the kitchen, in full view, like an idiot.

Reid sighed. *Will that boy never learn caution?* The good news was his cousin didn't end up with some holes in his torso—his aunt would have skinned him alive if her baby boy came to harm. Bad news was they'd lost their one lead to whoever was behind the random attacks.

Although, at least now Reid had confirmation. These *were* attacks. Someone was after his position as alpha of his clan. Someone was determined to undermine his authority. To try and take what was his. *Like fuck.*

He'd find out who the bastard was. Hunt him down like the vermin he was and exterminate him. Weak indeed. Reid would show him what happened when you poked a Kodiak with a stick.

"Boris, get rid of the body. Brody, take my idiot cousin and see if you can't find the sharpshooter who took out our friend here."

"You really think we'll find them?"

"No. Whoever took that shot was using a long-range rifle. You can tell by the wound and the lack of sound when they fired. I'll wager they're long gone."

"Then why bother?"

"Because I said so." And for retaliation over the wide-ass remark.

"What about you? What are you doing?"

"City girl and I have unfinished business."

Brody let out a low whistle. "Do you think that's wise?"

No. Probably not. But Reid was past caring. Being an alpha meant putting the needs and welfare of the clan above his own. But, for one night, just one, Reid was going to indulge in a selfish whim. A whim that involved him, a certain city girl, and lots of skin-to-skin touching.

Chapter Seventeen

After Reid left her with his ominous last words, Tammy paced her room.

What does he mean we're not done? Not done talking? Not done discussing his special affliction? Not done making out and having a wondrously sexy time?

The not knowing practically drove her crazy. She should march downstairs and confront him. Demand some answers!

She didn't leave her room. Already she was dealing with too much whacky shit. She really didn't need anything new to handle, not now.

But how could she extricate herself from the situation? She was here to do a job, a job as yet unfinished. Her boss was expecting a full report. What could she say? *No signs of foul play, but by the way, our client is a giant bear.*

He'd have her placed on stress leave in a heartbeat.

I could lie. It wouldn't be hard for her to claim she found no sign of foul play. Let the claims go through. However, if the problems persisted, then what?

Was there no solution to her dilemma? And what exactly was going on downstairs? A little while ago, she could have sworn she'd heard a man scream. Did she want to know for sure?

Not really. Just like she wished she could forget the disturbing sight of the bear who wasn't a bear. The man who wasn't a man. The kiss that was more than a kiss.

"Why so anxious?"

Reid's softly murmured query brought a shriek to her lips. She whirled, one hand clutching her chest where her heart pulsed double time. "Would you stop sneaking up on me!"

He arched a brow as his lips curved into a much-too-sexy grin. "And miss the opportunity for you to inflict damage? I have to say, I'm surprised. Not a single blow. I expected you to brain me with a lamp or a hairbrush at the very least."

"Don't tempt me."

"Someone's testy."

"Someone's really confused."

"Welcome to the club."

She frowned at him. "What do you have to be confused about? You're not the one who's suddenly discovered werebears exist and who had someone threaten to cook them if she didn't keep her mouth shut." Tammy still hadn't figured out if his grandmother meant it or not.

"I was shot. Or have you conveniently forgotten?"

"You're just never going to let me live that one down, are you?"

"Nope. But you can try and make amends." He took a step forward.

She refused to let him intimate her. With her chin tilted at a stubborn angle, she held her ground. "How?" Would he demand she falsify her report to her boss?

"I can think of a pleasurable way."

His innuendo made her eyes widen. Her pulse went from rapid to erratic, and she moistened her lips. He reached for her, but she evaded his grasp. She knew what would happen if he touched her, and yet, despite her head telling her to stay out of reach, her body reacted. Her breath came more raggedly, her nipples tightened, and warmth pooled between her thighs.

But as much as she might find his brand of ruggedness attractive, she wasn't about to just swoon in his arms—even if those big brawny arms could more than handle her plush curves. "Your grandmother's right. We shouldn't be doing this. It isn't right. I'm here to do a job, and that job doesn't involve doing you."

"What's happening between us has nothing to do with the insurance claim, and you know it."

"Then what does it have to do with?"

"You really have to ask?"

"Yes. Because I don't get it." Reid could have his pick of women. Sexy, poised, slim women like Jan. Why would he go after the chubby one who'd attacked him with a frying pan and shot him in the ass?

"You want me to say it out loud? Fine. You're mouthy, violent, and human, all things I should avoid, and yet, I can't help but want you."

"Gee, don't I feel all warm and fuzzy inside?" she said with evident sarcasm.

"You should take it as a compliment. It's not something I've ever had happen to me before. I'm usually much more picky about my bedmates."

"You mean you're used to skinnier, prettier ones."

The shock on his face wasn't feigned, and his words rang with sincerity. "You did not seriously just say that. For one thing, I like a woman in my bed. Not a stick. And we both know you're cute as a snow bunny with your big brown eyes."

"A bunny?"

"You're right. Too gentle. More like a lynx, wily and violent when threatened. Make no mistake. I'm attracted to you. I want to explore your curves. Rub myself against your skin. Make your body flush with passion."

"You speak as if we're going to have sex, and yet, I'm telling right now, it won't happen." Yup, she said it, and yet even she didn't truly believe it. She knew her body was more than willing. Then again, what woman wouldn't react to a virile, handsome man declaring his attraction?

"Give me a few more minutes. You'll be singing a different tune."

"I won't become your lover."

"Yet."

"Ever."

His confident smile called her a liar.

She shook her head. "You are being really stubborn. Not to mention unethical. How can I properly do my job if I'm sleeping with you?"

"Is that all that's stopping you? Then fine. I withdraw my claims."

Her jaw dropped. "You can't do that."

"I can and will if that's what it takes."

Surely he jested. What man gave up a fortune to spend the night with her? "Stop joking."

"No joke. I wasn't kidding when I said I wanted you. If your only objection is your ability to provide an unbiased report, then fine. No report needed. I won't follow through on the claim."

"You can't do that. It'll make you look suspicious. Like you know what's going on."

"I do. A rival is making a bid for my territory." He said it with nonchalance as he stripped his shirt off.

It took her a moment to regain her wits, as so much flesh bared all at once addled her. "I don't understand. What do you mean someone's after your territory?"

"It's simple. I am the head of this town. Clan. Company. Whatever you want to call it. I run it. I make the rules. I enforce them. In my world, that gives me the title of Alpha."

"So you're the big boss."

"Exactly. In shifter society, if someone thinks they have the strength, or if they get greedy, then they can make a move on a clan, either by outright challenge to the alpha or by striking out at them. In other words, doing things that will weaken the alpha's position and his pack."

His words reminded her of what his grandmother said earlier. "Kind of like sleeping with me would also weaken you."

"Says who?"

"Your grandmother. Isn't that what she meant earlier when she was reminding you of your position?"

He grimaced. "More or less. As alpha, I'm expected to marry for political reasons. To form an alliance with another clan."

"In other words, stick to your own kind."

"Yes. But, until then, that doesn't mean I can't take a lover, even a human one."

"So you want me to sleep with you, knowing we don't have a future." Well, she couldn't berate him for being honest. At least, unlike most men, he didn't pretend.

"We won't be doing much sleeping." His words, almost purred, sent a shiver through her that had nothing to do with the temperature in the room. Unless the heat in her body counted.

"What you're suggesting is—"

"A no-strings, no-promises evening of pleasure. Make that days, until you have to return to your life back in the city."

"That sounds so … tawdry." And exciting. What he suggested, on the one hand, was to treat her like some sort of sex kitten, a mistress for his pleasure. It was oddly arousing. Tammy had never had a man so openly proposition her before. A man who wanted her, at any cost, because he found her sexy.

If words could stroke, his did, and her body reacted. Could he sense it? Smell it? His nostrils did flare, and she could have sworn his eyes flashed. The animal within him reacting to her evident desire?

"At our core, human or bear, we both have needs. Carnal hungers. There is nothing wrong with feeding that hunger."

What he suggested, no strings, no emotional attachments, no expectations, was it something she should even contemplate? In a sense, he offered her the perfect solution. Indulge in the arousal, get it out of her system, then leave. Still, though, there was a name for girls who had sex just for the sake of it. "I don't kno—"

"You think and talk too much," he growled, cutting her off. In the blink of an eye, he'd closed the gap between them and taken her into his arms. His mouth claimed hers in a torrid kiss, one that wiped away her silly rebuttals.

Who was she kidding? She could argue until she turned blue. The simple fact of the matter was she did want Reid. Bear or not, he brought her body to life and made her blood boil in a way she'd never imagined. Yes, there was a chance she'd get her heart broken. Been there, done that, and she'd survived. But could she live with the regret of wondering what it could have been like? To always wonder if she'd missed out on the best experience of her life, however fleeting?

I can't. She wanted this. Needed this. Needed him.

Accepting it unleashed something within her. Her entire stance softened as she threw herself wholeheartedly into the embrace. If he noticed the difference, he didn't protest, but she could have sworn he grunted in approval.

With his big body wrapped around hers, it proved simple for him to maneuver her toward the bed until the backs of her legs hit the mattress. She tumbled onto it, losing his mouth in the process. But she didn't mourn its loss, not when it went in search of other places to kiss, like her neck, which led him to travel lower until the neckline of her shirt got in his way. Whoops. No it wasn't. In a deft motion, he'd yanked the offending garment off her, baring her to his view.

With the lights on in the bedroom, there was no hiding her lily-white skin, the roundness of her belly, or the ugly practical sports bra holding her heavy breasts in place.

But the sight seemed to enflame him, or so his guttural, "delicious", seemed to indicate. His lips pressed to her exposed flesh, exploring the valley between her breasts, while his hands fumbled at the clasp to her bra.

"Need some help?" she teased.

"No," was his disgruntled reply. "Stupid contraption." His solution? With a wrench, he forcibly snapped the clasp and peeled the offensive item from her.

"Hey, I happened to like that bra."

"I'll buy you another one. Hell, I'll buy you ten if you promise not to wear them around me."

"You want me to let the twin peaks swing free?" she said, her words ending on a gasp as his lips tugged at first one nipple then the other.

"Yes, or you'll end up with a pile of useless fabric."

She giggled at his vehemence, a sound that turned into a moan as he suckled at her erect tip. His hot mouth engulfed her breast, the sucking and tugging sending a jolt of pure pleasure to her sex. She writhed upon the mattress, apparently too much, because he settled his large body between her legs, pinning her.

She wrapped her legs around him, barely. Good thing she was tall or they wouldn't have fit. He was a big man. A solid man. A man who was slowly working his way lower, his hot mouth leaving a blazing trail in its wake as he edged closer and closer to the waistband of her slacks.

He managed the button and zipper on those without damage, and in short order, they went flying over his shoulder, leaving Tammy wishing she'd packed nicer underwear. Pink cotton panties did not scream seduction. As if he noticed. His mouth continued its descending exploration, nuzzling the fabric covering her sex then wetting it as he opened his mouth as if to take a bite. He didn't chomp down, but he did blow, warm, moist air.

She cried out and grabbed at his hair, her fingers tugging at the strands as she bucked against his sensual torture.

When he peeled her panties off, she was more than ready for his mouth to claim her sex, his tongue delving between her plump nether lips and lapping at the entrance of her pussy. A shudder went through her, and her channel tightened and clenched, eager for something to hold on to.

But he didn't give her what her sex so ardently wanted. Not yet. Instead, his tongue switched tactics, applying itself to her clitoris.

She yelled as he licked it and clasped it with his lips, the direct stimulation all her body needed to get pushed over the edge. An edge he seemed intent on shoving her off, again. He would not stop. In the throes of a climax that he just wouldn't allow to stop, she finally had to plead, "Enough!"

"Oh no, city girl, we're not done yet," he growled. Somehow during his oral assault of her tender parts, he'd lost his pants. Or so the probing head of his shaft indicated as he braced himself over her with arms corded with muscle. His lips caught hers, the taste of her still flavoring them, and she cried against his mouth as he penetrated her still-quivering sex, the thickness of him exactly what her body craved.

Big, so big and yet she stretched to accommodate him. But it was a tight fit. He grunted as he wiggled his way in until he was fully and firmly seated. Then he paused and said the most incongruous, and yet sweetest, thing, "Are you okay?"

Chapter Eighteen

Reid didn't understand her soft laughter at his query. He was well aware his large girth could cause discomfort. He did his best to ensure she was fully prepared for him, but at the same time, he remained—if barely—aware of her humanity and her more fragile nature.

Fragile and yet with a courage forged of steel. She was also, despite her silly doubts, a perfect-sized girl with curves that delighted him, a wanton desire to match his own, and a heavenly taste.

But she was also tight. Oh so very pleasurably tight. Enjoyable as he found that, he retained enough wits to make sure she was comfortable with the way he surely stretched her.

"I'm more than okay," she purred against his lips as her fingers threaded through his hair. As if to prove her statement, her hips undulated, drawing him impossibly farther in, and her sex must have enjoyed it because it quivered and squeezed

It was his turn to gasp, and his head bowed until his forehead touched hers. Without further words, they began to move, him thrusting in and out with long, slow strokes while she arched her hips, tilting them in such a way as to allow him deeper access. He knew he'd gotten the right angle to hit her sweet spot by the way her channel milked him like a vise each time he slammed his way in.

Her fingers stopped their painful tug, a pain he welcomed as a sign of her ardent arousal, and clutched at his shoulders. Her legs were wrapped around his waist, ankles locked, the strength in them welcome, as she seemed determined to hold onto him as fervently as he clung to her.

Together they moved in rhythm, their hearts racing in time, their ragged breathing matching up, and when their climax claimed them? They both yelled out, his body bowing in one mighty thrust, her body arching as her channel convulsed.

And in that one glorious moment, Reid knew he was in trouble. Big trouble. It didn't stop him from cradling the panting body of his city girl, of staying wrapped around her even as she fell asleep in his arms. He couldn't leave her side. Not only was his bear determined to remain close at hand to protect her, he wanted to stay.

So he stayed and screw anyone who didn't like it. *I'm the fucking alpha, and if I want to spend the night with a human I will.*

But of course his actions didn't go unnoticed or unchallenged.

The following morning, as a blushing Tammy finally left bed, sated, sticky, and in search of a hot shower, Reid took a quick sluice of his own before heading downstairs to face a bear who, while not bigger in size, definitely tried to tower over him in attitude and spirit.

His grandmother boldly stared at him as he entered the kitchen, the wooden spoon in her hand—the sturdy kind that didn't easily break off when applied to a naughty cub's butt—held high. "You spent the night with her." Stated not asked.

"I did."

"Was that wise?"

Nope. Pleasurable? Yes. "I don't see what wisdom has to do with me having sex with someone I find attractive."

"Don't get smart-mouthed with me, Reid Carver. I've got a spoon, and I'm not afraid to use it." Especially since she knew he wouldn't do a thing to protect himself.

His parents and grandmother had raised him to never lift a hand against a woman and, most especially, not against his beloved Ursa.

"What do you want me to tell you? There's something about her that I can't help but crave." Problem was, despite their night of pleasure, the craving remained. He'd thought by the third time he claimed her willing body he'd have regained some measure of control. Instead, it seemed his hunger for her had deepened.

His grandmother sighed. "Believe it or not, I do understand. She's different than the women you're used to seeing every day, and she's got a strong character. I can understand your attraction even if I don't condone it. Please tell me you at least used protection?"

No, he hadn't. He'd not even thought to bring condoms to her room. Didn't pull out. Didn't take any of his usual precautions. He would have liked to blame his frazzled mental state, maybe even his bear, which had pretty much run the show, but no, a part of him had known what he did. Known and didn't care. But he wasn't about to admit that to his Ursa. So he adopted an affronted and embarrassed tone. "I am not discussing my sex life with you. Suffice it to say, you've nothing to worry about." Tammy was a city girl. Chances were she was on the pill.

And if she's not? The thought of her belly swelling with his child—*my cub*—didn't send him into a blind panic. Not like he had when he thought he'd gotten his college girlfriend knocked up.

What did that mean? Was he ready to perhaps settle down and start a family? He thought of various alpha daughters paraded past him over the years. Most attractive and intelligent. None made him want to rush out and hitch a knot. On the contrary, he grimaced. And yet, when he thought of the tousled-haired human upstairs? He wanted to race back to her side and make love to her until she let out that soft moan that meant he'd hit her sweet spot.

"You want to sow some oats, fine. Get her out of your system, but don't forget who you are. It is one thing to dally with a human, but you're alpha to this clan. You have responsibilities to those you protect and lead. A duty to your name. Don't let lust cloud your judgment."

"I won't." Yet he already had. "And you don't have to worry. She won't be here much longer. Now that I know someone's making a bid for power, I'm going to have her chalk up the missing trucks to driver and mechanical error. The trailers as crimes of opportunity. We'll swallow the financial loss and make sure future shipments are better guarded until I hunt down the culprit and take care of him and his bid to undermine me."

Her shrewd blue gaze pinned him. "So when the time comes, you'll let her walk away?"

No. Oops, the word almost slipped past his lips. It definitely rang in his head as his bear answered. But Reid knew where his duty resided. He'd do the right thing, even if it fucking killed him. *Don't I always?*

Chapter Nineteen

Tammy dithered in her bedroom. Showered, dressed, and out of things to do, she hesitated before leaving the safety of her quarters. She feared facing Reid's grandmother. Especially since the old woman probably knew where Reid spent the night—and what they'd done.

I wasn't exactly quiet. Then again, neither was he. The man practically roared when he came. Sexy at the time, not so sexy with the realization they might have been heard.

On the heels of facing the old woman was that of facing Reid. Sexy, glorious Reid, who made her see stars, fireworks, and the realization that not all men were the same when it came to pleasure in the bedroom. Not even close.

Sex with Reid was on a level she never imagined. And his unexpected tenderness as he cradled her, kissed her flushed cheeks, stroked her gently with calloused fingers? A girl could all too easily fall in love. A big no-no. He'd said it himself. He wasn't meant for her. She wasn't meant for him. He belonged to this town, this place and she … she just didn't.

But back to her first dilemma. How to face the day without dying of embarrassment.

With warm cheeks and downcast eyes, Tammy slunk into the kitchen and practically flinched when Ursula greeted her with a warm, "Good morning. Did you sleep well?"

Sleep? *Didn't do much of that.* "Um, yeah." Her reply had Reid, who was sipping on a cup of coffee, shaking with suppressed laughter. It seemed he'd not run off to the office this morning but stuck around. *For me?* So the subtle caress of his hand on her waist seemed to indicate when she took the stool beside him.

After that first awkward moment, things returned to normal, normal if she ignored the fact Reid was a bear, his grandmother probably one too, and the fact she'd slept with him. Ooh, then add to that the attempted home invasion-kidnapping attempt. It took two cups of coffee before she felt her nerves smooth out enough to ignore the taped cardboard in the kitchen door—but nothing could stop the tingles of his touch.

It was decided, by Reid no less—*Mr. Bossypants*, which wouldn't last long once she got a private moment—that Tammy was best off remaining with him for safety reasons, but not before he'd dropped his grandmother off at a family member's house, despite her protests.

"I've been taking care of myself since before you were born," his grandmother argued as he plucked her from his truck and carted her to the front door of a house in town.

"Yup. I know. You fought off trappers and settlers and the Abominable Snowman too. I get it. But humor me and stay with Auntie Jean, would you, while I go to work? I'd feel better knowing they had you on hand in case something happens. You know how Auntie Jean is with guns."

Sly, but effective. By implying his aunt needed protection, he ended up giving his grandmother purpose and diffusing her arguing.

"That was slick," Tammy said when he clambered back into the truck.

"Yet necessary. Sometimes my grandmother doesn't realize she's almost seventy years old. The idea of letting others care for her is like a vile sentence."

"You don't think she really fell for the whole protect-your-aunt bit, do you?"

"No, but it helps her save face. She might not admit it, but the fact someone was brazen enough to try and invade our home last night while I was away freaked her out. Else there's no way I would have gotten her stubborn ass into my truck."

"She's lucky to have you."

"No, I'm lucky to have her. Ursa practically raised me and then kind of took over my care after my parents death."

"Did you lose them young?"

"Not really. I was almost twenty-five when the avalanche buried them."

Tammy winced. "I'm sorry."

"Accidents happen. Time heals most wounds. That was almost seven years ago."

"So you inherited the company from your dad?"

"Yeah and my position as alpha. It meant getting a discharge from the army but—"

"You were in the army?" She couldn't hide her surprise.

"Yeah."

"But, you're a bear. Weren't you afraid they'd, you know, notice you were different?"

"My entire platoon was shifter-based. While the world might not know about us, the military and the government has for years. The battlefield isn't a place you can easily hide your beast side."

"Then why go and put yourself in that position?"

"Young predators, especially ones with alpha tendencies, need an outlet. Put too many of us in one place without a way to expend our energy and you can end up with some serious aggression problems. It's why so many of us choose to serve a few years in the military. Their conditioning and a few missions into hostile territory are great lessons when it comes to control. Not to mention, it helps us appreciate our home that much more."

"So you served in the war overseas?"

"I did my part. Many of us did. But it's not something we talk about much. War isn't pretty. Or glamorous."

"Thank you."

He shot her a look as he drove. "Thank you for what?"

"For serving our country. For volunteering to make a difference."

A crooked grin lit his face with a boyishness she found much too endearing. "You're welcome. And tell you what, if you want to thank me again later, I've got a scar or two you can kiss better."

"Men! Does everything have to revolve back to sex?"

"Yes."

She laughed. After that, their talk turned to more banal matters, such as the size of the town and its amenities. Despite her city living, Tammy couldn't deny a certain appeal to living somewhere where everyone literally said hello to you by name. A small town might mean everyone stuck their noses in your business; however, given the level of camaraderie she'd seen and affection amongst the people she met, it didn't seem to bother anyone much.

Once they arrived at the office, before Reid abandoned her for his office, he made her promise to meet him for lunch, and despite Jan watching, he dropped a light kiss on her lips. Silly, but it warmed her right down to her wooly-sock-covered toes.

Left to her own devices, Tammy ended up in the garage where a truck was parked with its hood up. She couldn't have said what she hoped to find. Reid had confirmed the missing trucks and trailers weren't accidents but the act of some rival. Technically that meant their disappearance fell under the heading of theft, but how could she incorporate that into her paperwork without revealing the odd politics and the town's even odder circumstances? A bigger dilemma was given she knew there was nothing left to investigate, she could technically leave anytime.

She just didn't want to. *Which means I have to.*

No girl ever set out to be that pathetic one who whined and cried and held on longer than she should. The rules of the game were clear. No strings, no emotions, just sex. Great sex. An incredible guy. A bear. A bear who was expected to hook up with someone of his own kind.

Not me.

She needed to make plans to leave.

As she sauntered closer to the truck under repair, she ran into Travis. He tossed her a cocky grin. "Heard you had a bit of excitement last night."

For a second, she wondered if everyone knew she'd slept with Reid, but then she caught on to what he meant. It didn't stop her cheeks from heating though. "Just a little." More like a lot. The trip had opened her eyes—and senses—to much more than she'd expected.

"Did you really shoot Reid in the ass? And then threaten him with a frying pan?"

She almost winced as she said, "Yes."

Travis practically doubled over in laughter. "Oh, I wish someone had caught that on video. My big and growly cousin, taken down by a city girl armed with a non-stick pan."

"Actually, I grabbed the cast iron one. It has more weight."

He laughed even harder.

Given what she knew now of Reid and many of the town's inhabitants, she eyed Travis, wondering if he was also a bear beneath his friendly, human demeanor. And what about scowling Boris, whom she now suspected had put her to sleep less by accident and more to ensure she didn't witness something she shouldn't have?

So many secrets this town hid. It worried her that given the level of violence she'd seen and heard of so far that, when the time came for her to leave, her knowledge might hamper her. *Will Reid try and stop me?* Would she stay if he asked?

As if he'd ask. That man would order her and expect her to obey. Like that would happen, although it did raise an interesting dilemma. What if, say, Reid did ask her to stick around, not because of any secret, but because he genuinely wanted her to? He'd admitted himself he couldn't help but crave her. The night they'd spent proved that and then some. But he'd also made it clear there was no future for them together. So, by staying, she would, in effect, set herself up for heartbreak, and the deeper she got entrenched in his town's problems, and secrets, the less likely they'd just let her go.

A theory reinforced when she ran into Jan just before lunch.

"So I hear you and the boss are an item. Given you probably didn't pack for an extended stay, I contacted a cousin who's about your size, and she's going to send over some extra clothes."

"Who said I was staying longer?"

Jan's smile faded. "You and Reid hooked up."

"Kind of, but it was just a casual thing. I'm still planning to go home. At this point, probably the sooner the better."

"Sooner?" Reid's deep baritone sent an excited quiver through her, and Tammy turned to see him silhouetted in his office door.

Tammy shrugged. "There's really no reason for me to stay." Other than to indulge in melt-your-socks sex.

"I see," was his tight-lipped reply. "Jan, could you excuse me and Tammy? I'd like to speak with her. Oh, and hold any calls or visitors. I don't want to be interrupted."

He didn't give Tammy a chance to refuse, grasping her by the arm and practically hauling her inside before slamming the door shut and locking it.

"Is there a problem?" she asked. She licked her lips as she looked at him. Her heart raced faster, not in fear despite the scowl on his face. Angry or happy, Reid was delicious.

"Yes, there's a problem. You can't leave yet."

"Why not? You didn't steal the shipments, and I got an email from my boss about twenty minutes ago saying my job here is done."

"There's been a development in the case. The trucks and trailers were recovered this morning. A little worse for wear, and empty of cargo, but intact."

"What about the drivers?"

The bleak look on his face said it all.

"I'm sorry."

"Don't be. Their families will have vengeance." His dark tone rang with deadly promise.

She shivered. "So I guess since the investigation is back on with the authorities, I should pack my things and find out when I can hitch a ride back to the airport then."

"Not yet. It's too dangerous. We haven't yet caught whoever's responsible."

"I can't stay here forever. I've got a job to go back to. A life."

"It's not safe."

Why did a part of her hope to hear the words, *"Because I don't want you to go. I need you. Stay with me."* One night of sex didn't give her a right to expect those words. It didn't stem the disappointment. Her chin tilted at a stubborn angle. "I'm going back, and you can't stop me."

"Are you really challenging me on this?" His eyes flashed, a glint of gold and wildness that made her heart rate increase. "You'll go when I say you can."

"You can't keep me a prisoner."

"I can do anything I want. I own this town. If I spread the word that you're not to be given a ride back to the city, do you really think anyone will gainsay me?"

"Why are you doing this?" *Tell me it's because you want me. Tell me you've changed your mind and you want to see if we belong together.*

"I need to protect my clan, and in order to do that, you have to stay until I know that I can trust you."

"Trust me?" She gaped at him. "Did you seriously just say that?"

"I have to do what's best—"

She cut him off. "Don't feed me that line of crap. You're a bully."

"I'm assertive."

"I won't have you giving me orders."

"You will obey me on this." He stepped into her space and tried to stare her down.

She met his gaze. Big, bad bear or not, she wasn't about to let him cow her. "I'm going home."

"No." He grabbed at her, his hands rough at her waist as he drew her to him for a punishing kiss. But the ferocity of it thrilled her. His words might say one thing, but his kiss, oh my his kiss, said something else.

Despite her anger at him, with him and with herself for her weakness, she couldn't help but melt in his embrace. What was it about him that blasted all her good intentions?

As his hands roamed her body, she couldn't help but relax and mold herself to him, pressing the aching tips of her breasts against his rock-hard chest, angling her hips to feel the firm rigidity of his cock against her lower belly, a symbol that their kiss affected him just as greatly.

She forgot not only her irritation with him; she forgot where they were. That they had an audience right outside his office door.

As if they played a role in a romantic movie, he literally swept half of his desk clean, sending papers and folders, even pens, tumbling to the floor, clearing a spot so he could sit her on the scarred wooden surface. She wondered why for a moment until he began yanking at her pants, tugging them past her hips and buttocks down her legs. He stripped them off her, leaving her clad only in her shirt and socks, in too much of a hurry it seemed to go any further.

He dropped to his knees between her thighs, a supplicant determined to pay homage on a certain part of her body. At the first lick of his tongue across her nether lips, she couldn't help but cry out. She quickly bit her lip, using the sharp point of pain to muffle further sounds, trying to keep the audible evidence of her pleasure quiet. But he made it so hard. He feasted on her, spreading her plump lips to lap at her core. He jabbed her with his tongue. He flicked her clit. He sucked on it. Toyed with her as she leaned back on his desk, panting and quickly approaching the edge of pleasure.

But he didn't let her come. Not yet.

Grasping her by the thighs, he slid her off the desk and spun her. A firm hand in the middle of the back bent her over, and she placed her hands flat on the wooden surface as he nudged her thighs apart. The distinctive sound of a zipper lowering preceded the poke of his hard cock against her moist sex.

He didn't fumble or play around. He thrust into her welcoming channel. Slid his thick shaft into her, stretching her. He curled an arm around her waist as he leaned over her. His other hand palmed the desk as a brace. Positioned, he began to pump her, in and out strokes, deep, hard, and oh so welcome.

Her sex clung to his cock, squeezing and fisting it, shuddering each time he struck her inner sweet spot. Faster he thrust, in and out, his breathing just as ragged as her own, his arm tight around her waist so as to not lose his rhythm.

When she came, a climax that wrung his name from her in a tortured gasp, he growled, a soft rumble, which only made her shudder harder.

But it was his huskily said, "*mine!*" that triggered her second orgasm.

Their breathing erratic, her heart racing, and her body now limp, she remained bent over his desk, his body curved against her backside. She could have stayed like this forever. All it would take was a few words. The right words.

But being a man, he, of course, didn't say them. Instead he showed his cave bear roots.

"You're staying, and that's final."

We'll see about that.

Chapter Twenty

Reid felt the anger in Tammy not even a second after he spoke. Saw it in the way her lips remained tight and her glances glared. In silence, she dressed.

Let her be angry. She'd come to understand he did it for her own good.

Hers or mine? he wondered as she slammed out of his office in a huff.

The more Tammy seemed determined to leave, the more Reid didn't want to let her go. Part of it had to do with her safety like he'd mentioned. Another with the fact that she knew his secret, the town's secret really, and he was somewhat worried about it getting out. But the real reason, the biggest one, was he didn't want her to leave. *She can't leave me.*

Yeah, he knew she wasn't the woman for him. He understood she belonged to a different world than his. Yet, it didn't change how he felt, and he couldn't even blame it all on his bear.

I want her to stay. With me. She's mine. Even if she refused to recognize it.

The more she argued about wanting to go, the more adamant he became about making her stay. The more her eyes flashed and she tilted that stubborn chin, as she faced him, unafraid and sexy, the more he wanted to crush her perfect frame to his and kiss those delectable lips until they changed their tune.

It was why he couldn't stop himself. Why he took her over his desk, her sweet ass a welcome cushion for his pushing. He thrust into her welcoming heat until the defiance in her turned to soft cries of "yes". No matter those yeses were for something else, they appeased his inner beast.

But they didn't solve his dilemma.

How to keep her? Not now. She'd stalked off in a snit, a probably deserved one given his high handedness with her, but what else could he do? She wanted to leave, and for some reason, he just couldn't let that happen. Yet she was right. She couldn't stay forever, not unless he did something to make her situation more permanent.

If he claimed her as mate, he'd cause a shitstorm with his grandmother, his family, hell, possibly the whole town, who expected their alpha to choose a shifter to stand at his side. Custom and expectation, though, didn't take into account his happiness. His wants. *My needs.*

He was boss, Alpha and leader. If he wanted to keep Tammy by his side, did he really give a flying fuck what the rest of the world thought? What was the point of having all this power, of ensuring he had the respect of his clan, if not to use it? Yes, taking a human as mate might be selfish, but dammit, the world wouldn't end if he indulged in one selfish act. Yes, he might have to face some grumbles and disappointment, but fuck it. Being a leader wasn't about making everyone happy but about doing what was right. And what was right for him had stalked out of his office and was threatening to escape from his life.

Not acceptable. I'm keeping her.

However, how could he convince her to stay, and stay not because of danger or because he'd accused her of not being trustworthy? How did he get her to agree and have her feel for him what he felt for her?

They'd known each other for only a few days. No way would she understand that shifters were more impulsive and intuitive when it came to selecting a mate. Humans had all these strange preconceived notions about dating and compatibility. Hell, they even had quizzes in those girly magazines sold on the shelves at the store.

Reid didn't need no stupid multiple-choice questionnaire to tell him he and Tammy were compatible. He knew it. Felt it.

He'd have to figure out a solution to his dilemma later, though. For the moment, she was stuck because he'd not lied about that. If he said no one would give her ride, then no amount of bribery would change anyone's mind.

Once he got back from his planned ambush, he'd work on convincing her. First, he had some murdering little bastards to take care of.

Boris and the others had fixed the transport truck's radiator problem. Reid had finagled a load to appease one of his distributors, and Travis was prepping to leave tonight with Boris, while Reid, Brody, and a bunch of others would shadow them on snowmobiles. If trouble dared attack—and he hoped they did—they'd have a surprise.

As for Tammy, his grandmother, and the town? Reid figured there was safety in numbers. For the night, his Ursa could stay at his Aunt Jean's house and Tammy would bunk at Jan's, whose collection of firearms could probably stall a small army. His receptionist might appear sophisticated on the outside, but the girl had a fetish for weapons rivalled only by Boris.

And if all went well, in twenty-four hours, Reid would have taken care of the threat to his position, avenged his people, and he could concentrate on convincing one sexy city girl that she wanted to relocate—permanently.

Chapter Twenty-one

Tammy mumbled under her breath as she paced Jan's pristine living room. Forget rustic country style, the room could have been taken straight from a home décor magazine for modern perfection. White walls, dark floors, and creamy-colored chenille couches with a matching beige rug were highlighted by brilliant red pillows and colorful artwork on the walls depicting, of all things, quaint Paris side streets and the waterways of Venice.

"Stupid stubborn bear thinks he can tell me what to do." Tammy still couldn't believe the nerve of him. She'd foolishly expected, after their tryst, for him to declare something, affection, or even a plea for her to stay so they could explore this wild attraction between them. Instead, he pulled an I-am-the-boss bullshit thing, an attitude that he then expanded upon when he told her in no uncertain terms that she would be spending the night and possibly the next day with Jan while he took care of business. In other words, hunted down the guy screwing with his business and threatening his family.

Fine. She could understand he felt a need to handle things and that he was concerned for her safety. However, it was how he did it. He didn't ask. He ordered. Hot when done in the bedroom and during sex, not so hot when Tammy was mad and wanted to flee for home where she had ice cream in her freezer perfect for a wounded heart.

As if dealing with her tumultuous emotions wasn't enough, he took her phone! Took it and forbade Jan from letting her use one.

Tammy finally relented in her angry silent treatment to ask, "Why can't I use a phone? I need to call my office and let them know I'm going to be delayed for a few days. And what about my mother? She gets worried when I don't check in." Or if she didn't answer. Or if the moon and Saturn were in a certain position in the sky. Her mother had issues when it came to Tammy's safety. But Tammy forgave them, given what had happened to her dad, the one and only love of her mother's life.

Reid's reply. "I'll take care of it."

Her cold shoulder after that didn't stop him from dropping a heart-stopping, heat-inducing whopper of a kiss on her lips. Then, he courted another frying pan to the head when he told her to, "Behave," before swatting her on the butt. She gaped, he grinned, completely unrepentant, and strode off—with an ass that was much too sexy for glaring at—to take care of "business."

Jan had to notice Tammy's less-than-happy demeanor, but she didn't say much, not during the ride to her place. But that changed once they got to her bungalow.

"So what are you going to do?" Jan asked as she stripped out of her outerwear and hung it on a coat rack just inside the door.

"What do you mean?"

"I couldn't help but overhear Reid. He's forbidden you from leaving."

"Apparently he has *trust* issues." Tammy made some air quotes as she rolled her eyes. "Like I'd go blabbing his secret or yours to anyone else. I prefer a room without padded walls, thank you very much."

"Maybe it's his man-way of asking you to stay."

"I doubt it. He's made it pretty clear that I'm too human for him. Apparently, I'm good enough for a wham-bam thank you ma'am, but anything else is out of the question."

"Ouch."

"Not really. He was pretty upfront from the get go about it."

"Do you like him?"

"Yes and no. I mean I'm attracted to him, and I think under the right circumstances we could make things work. But he's not interested in that, and I am not going to be one of those girls who begs or lets a man use her."

"So what are you going to do?"

Tammy shrugged. "What can I do for the moment? I want to leave. He won't let me. I guess I'm stuck for the moment."

"Or not." Jan went to a gleaming black armoire, which Tammy assumed hid her television and sound system. Wrong. The doors opened up onto a mini armory.

"Holy smokes. Why so many guns?" Tammy asked as she eyeballed the deadly stash.

"My dad liked them, and when I was young, he taught me to shoot. I hear you're a pretty good shot yourself."

"My father also had a thing for weapons."

"Had?"

"He died when I was just a kid."

"Sorry."

"Yeah, well, accidents happen." And the guilt never died. "But I don't understand why you're showing me this."

"You want to leave, right?"

"Yes. Haven't you heard, though? Reid won't let me."

"What if I could help you?"

A crease formed on her brow. "How?"

"I'll drive you, of course. The big rigs aren't the only way in and out of town. I've got all-wheel drive. Hell, we'll make better time in my SUV than in one of those big noisy trucks. But, if we're going to hit the road, we should bring along some protection just in case."

"You mean arm ourselves? Do you think we might be attacked?"

While Tammy got the feeling the stranger from the other night wouldn't be bothering her again, she couldn't ignore the fact that Reid thought the problems plaguing his town and clan weren't over.

"So far, they haven't targeted regular folk, but a girl can never be too cautious."

"What about Reid's ban on helping me leave? You do know he'll probably get mad."

"Yes he will." Jan shrugged. "He'll roar. I'll probably get reamed out and punished, but ultimately, he'll understand I'm doing this for his own good. For the town's sake."

"Because your alpha can't date a human."

"No, he could. He is the leader, and he could change the rules. But, let's be honest here, you don't belong here. He doesn't call you city girl for nothing. I don't mean for that to sound mean or disparaging. It's just life out here isn't for everyone. Heck, there are days I want to ditch the small-town life and move to the city." A wistful expression crossed Jan's face.

"Why don't you leave if you feel that way? You're smart and beautiful. Why not spread your wings or, er, paws and see what else it out there?"

A sad expression crossed Jan's face. "You make it sound so easy. Maybe it is for you."

Don't be so sure. I want to stay. Yet, as Reid and now Jan are telling me, I can't.

"In my case, I know for a fact my future is here, even if he won't recognize it." Jan sighed.

Sounded as if someone suffered from unrequited love. Tammy wondered who the guy was. But even more, she wondered if she had the guts to take Jan up on her offer. *Or should I give it a few more days and stay like Reid wants? I can't believe he doesn't feel anything for me. He's too tender. Too focused.* Too everything. He wasn't the type of man to indulge carelessly, and yet he had—with Tammy.

Did it mean something? And if it did…

Let's say he did ask her to stick around and see if they could try and build something together. Would she say yes? Could she?

Despite the initial culture shock, Tammy knew she could enjoy living in Kodiak Point. After the hustle of the city, quiet was proving nice. *Just think how relaxing it would be, especially if no one is shooting at me or trying to kidnap me.* It wouldn't take much to ditch her city girl nickname. Once upon a time, she'd loved the simpler life. Finding a job might prove challenging though.

Hold on, why was she thinking on such permanent terms? Safety concerns were why Reid didn't want her departing quite yet. Not because of anything else. Which meant no making of plans or looking for jobs. Her time here was temporary. Technically, it was over. So why was she hesitating over Jan's offer? Staying meant more of Reid, more of her heart getting lost, more pain when he did eventually tire of her and told her it was safe to go.

Sucking in a breath, Tammy made her choice. "Are we waiting for morning?"

Blonde hair swirled as Jan shook her head. "Why? It won't be any brighter outside. Let's get this done while Reid is busy. Actually, with the boys laying a trap with the truck, chances are we'll get a clean run into town and have you on a plane back home in no time."

A home without a bear.

Probably a good thing. Her nosy neighbor would surely call animal control.

Chapter Twenty-two

Wouldn't it figure he set a trap and no one stepped into it? Reid gunned his machine back toward his town—and Tammy.

He'd not received any texts or calls about attacks on the clan, yet that didn't lessen his haste. For once, he was eager to get home. There was someone he wanted to see.

See? Ha. He wanted to toss his city girl over a shoulder, swat her round ass if she protested—please let her protest—and cart her off to bed.

Except when he got home, pit stopping first at Jan's place, it was to find it dark and empty. He called around and ignored the grumbles of his bear. The first chill of something wrong didn't start until he realized no one had seen the women since they'd left the company offices the day before. Nor heard from them.

What started as a casual search expanded into a more organized one as he set off a firestorm of calls—courtesy of his Aunt Jean.

"Aunt Jean, I need to find Jan and Tammy. Can you locate them for me?"

A woman with a mission, Aunt Jean fired up the grapevine. Yet, for once, his gossipy aunt with her finger on the pulse of the town couldn't tell him anything other than Jan came home but left less than an hour later, with Tammy. And no one had seen them since. Over sixteen hours at this point.

Reid kind of lost it then and once his rampage was done, made a mental note to order a new chair for his grandmother. But his dilemma remained.

It didn't take a genius to figure out what happened. Jan, that vexing vixen, had taken Tammy away.

Away from me.

He'd kill her. No, he couldn't do that—people might get upset—but he could yell. And after he was done, he'd—

What? Go chasing after the human who evidently didn't want him? Drag his city girl back and, what, claim her?

"What are you doing standing here?" His grandmother's words arrived a second after the slap to the back of his head.

It didn't really sting, but he uttered a vehement, "ouch," anyway. "What was that for?"

"Are you truly that dense? Go after her."

"Who, Jan? I've already got the boys working on seeing if they can find her. Brody is going house to house in town just in case they went visiting, while Boris and Travis are combing the road heading into the city." Because he wouldn't put it past Jan to disobey him and take Tammy away. However, given their troubles, the fact Jan wasn't answering her phone could mean trouble.

"Go after Tammy, you idiot. I can see you want to."

"I'm alpha. I can't just go bearing off after a woman. She left. Which is for the best. Couldn't have the purists upset," he grumbled, unable to hide his discontent.

"Oh please, that handful of old geezers and biddies. Who cares what they think?"

"Says someone who is one of them. Since when do you want me to take up with her? Weren't you the one trying to remind me of duty?"

"Well, I couldn't just give you carte blanche to seduce the sweet girl. I was raised with morals you know."

He snorted. "Morals you call upon only when they suit you."

"Prerogative of age."

"Let me get this straight. Now you're telling me I should mate with a human? What happened to that pureblood crap?"

Ursa shrugged. "About that... Truth is the mixing of lines is a sometimes necessary thing. Too much inbreeding causes more harm than good. While not bandied about often, the shifter gene is pretty dominant when it comes to mixed pairings. Chances are any children you and Tammy would have would end up being a bear like its daddy. And if you want to be really sure, there's also the change. She's a tough girl. She'd probably survive it."

Tough, yes, but could he risk her life like that? It boiled down to whether he cared if all his progeny ended up cubs. Not really. Cub or not, he couldn't see himself not loving them. His grandmother's approval, though, didn't mean he let her off the hook that easily. Not after the blue-ball hell she'd put him through.

"Morals aside, if you think that I should keep Tammy, then why did you stop me the other night?"

His grandmother grinned. "Reverse psychology. Sometimes it takes being denied to recognize what you need and be willing to fight for it. Although, I am beginning to wonder. I truly never expected you'd actually let her go."

"I wasn't planning to," he admitted. "I'd hoped to have time to work on her under the guise of keeping her safe." While also apologizing for his actions. He'd acted pretty heavy handed.

Perhaps had I behaved a little less draconian, or should I say stubborn bear, she wouldn't have felt a need to flee. Given who raised him, and the strong women who populated his life, he should have known an ultimatum with someone like Tammy wouldn't go over well. Especially when coupled with his phone ban. He did feel kind of bad about blocking her from calling her mom, but in his defense, he'd not wanted her to cultivate an escape plan before he could get his chance at convincing her to stay.

"That girl was smitten with you, Reid Carver. It wouldn't have taken more than a few words to convince her to stay."

Words he still wasn't sure of. Could he offer his city girl a lifestyle she could handle? There was more than one reason why humans, and even outsiders, weren't considered perfect mates. Not everyone could handle the remoteness and lack of amenities of his town. Some started out fine but—

The theme song from an old cartoon titled *Rocky and Bullwinkle* interrupted from his front jean pocket.

Boris was calling. Reid answered. "Hey, moosehead. Got anything to report?"

Tone just as flat as ever, Boris said, "You need to get out here. The women never made it to town."

A cold chill froze his limbs as Reid asked, "What do you mean?"

"I'm about two hours from the ice gorge, by the ravine. I've found Jan's truck."

Reid's heart stopped as inside his mind his bear let out a mournful wail. "They're—"

"Not dead. But they are missing."

"How hard can they be to find?" Reid asked. "You should be able to track them by scent."

"I never said they'd be hard to find. However, given the number of snowmobile tracks, I might need a hand. Unless you'd like me to get all the glory."

Someone took his city girl? *My city girl? MINE!*

More bear than man, Reid growled, "I'm on my way."

And the fates help whoever took his Tammy because, once he got his paws on them, he would show no mercy. Especially if they'd hurt her.

Then they'll die.

Chapter Twenty-three

It didn't take long for Tammy to regret her choice. Only two hours of driving in the endless black and she fidgeted in her seat and kept glancing in the side view mirror, looking—hoping—for what?

Reid, of course. In her fantasy, he either chased them down, the winterized version of a biker wearing his black parka, shaded helmet, a growling sled between his powerful thighs. Or he tore after them as a bear. She all too easily dreamed up a big furry hairball, racing on all fours, roaring as he charged after their taillights.

I am such a contrary idiot. She argued with him about wanting to leave when he wouldn't let her go. And now that she'd escaped, she wanted him to fetch her back.

Being herself was sometimes way too complicated. She sighed.

Jan glanced over at her. "What's wrong?"

"Ever get the impression you made a huge mistake?"

"All the time. Then I pull out a gun and tell him to get dressed before I shoot his balls off."

It took Tammy a dropped-jaw moment before she realized Jan was teasing. The blonde laughed. "Oh, if you could only see your face right now. I'm just kidding. Mostly."

"I take it you're not dating right now."

"Nope. I know which man I want. I'm just waiting for him to get his head out of the sand and stop pretending he's not good enough for anyone."

"He's got issues?"

"Major ones." Jan blew out a breath. "Has since he came back from overseas. I know I should be patient, but it's costing me a fortune in batteries."

"Is he worth the wait?" Tammy asked.

A lilt of Jan's lips said yes. "Even if he is a stubborn idiot, yeah, he's worth it. But how did we get on the topic of me? I thought we were talking about you. About making a mistake. Let me guess. You want to go back."

Tammy scrunched up her nose. "I do. Does that make me the stupidest woman alive?"

Jan smiled and shook her head. "Nope, it means that, like I suspected, you do feel the bond with Reid."

"Bond? What bond?"

"There are times in a shifter's life when you run into a person and there's like a bolt of lightning. A sensation of rightness. Desire. Need."

"Extreme lust," Tammy joked, even as a part of her totally understood what Jan said. She couldn't deny something had happened to her the moment she met Reid.

"Lust is a part of it, yes, but the bond I'm talking about is on a wholly deeper level. We call this primal and overwhelming urge the mating instinct. It is quite the powerful force, and if those affected don't fight it, like someone I know," Jan muttered under her breath, "then it can lead to a fulfilling, lifelong commitment."

"And you think I have this mating thing going on for Reid?" They certainly had the horizontal tango down pat, along with a few other intimate dances.

"Not just you. Him too. I believe you're fated mates."

Tammy snorted. "I highly doubt it."

"Why? Humans fall in love at first sight all the time. Shifters kind of do the same, but it's more an instinct born of sight, scent, and some kind of metaphysical rightness, something I suspect we get from our animal side."

"Great, so his bear possibly thinks I'm a tasty treat."

A smile curved Jan's lips. "In a sense. But, again, it's more than that. Fated couples just mesh with each other. It's as if a higher power recognizes a compatible pair and moves events to ensure they cross paths."

"Or bonks him on the head," Tammy muttered.

"Or shoots him in the butt." Jan laughed. "The methods change with each couple."

How nice and romantic to think the universe was vested in her enough to show an interest in her love life. The cynical part of Tammy wanted to scoff—mock and, yeah, deride the whole concept. Another part, though, couldn't help a wistful, "So you think Reid and I are meant to be together?"

"Yes."

No hesitation. "And yet, if you're so sure, then why are you helping me to escape?"

"To make sure I was right. Given your humanity, I had to make certain it was more than just a case of you having the hots for the leader of our clan. Reid tends to have an effect on women."

"So I've noticed," Tammy replied, not without a tinge of jealousy as she wondered who else lusted after him.

"I'll admit I was beginning to second-guess myself until I saw you squirming the farther out we went."

"Could have been an urge to pee. I did drink a travel mug's worth of coffee."

"Do you have to pee?"

"No."

"Are you going to deny I'm right?"

Tammy sighed. "No. I can't help it. I know it's crazy to want to go back. I've got a mortgage, a job, friends back home, but a part of me, a big part is screaming at me to go back to Kodiak Point. Calling me an idiot, in fact, for running away from Reid." And what she suspected was a pivotal moment in her life, the moment that would decide the fate of her happiness.

"Minor details. The house can be rented or sold. I could use someone who knows her way around an office and a computer to help out, and as for friends, I'd like to count myself as one of the first of many in Kodiak Point."

"You make it sound easy." Tammy's heart thumped. Fear or exhilaration? "What if—"

A scream tore free from Tammy as Jan wrenched the wheel and sent them spinning on the icy surface, the tires and bumper slicing through a soft drift of snow, sending it scattering and whirling.

Holding on to the oh-shit bar, Tammy took a moment to recover before yelling, "What the hell?"

Jan laughed. "That's what I like to call a powder donut."

"You're crazy," Tammy muttered, but a smile curved her lips. "I like it."

"Crazy like a fox. Let's go home," Jan announced, shoving down hard on the gas pedal and sending her SUV rocketing, the tail end swerving a bit with the momentum.

With laughter and a much less stilted atmosphere, they headed back to Kodiak Point—to Reid. Tammy tried not to dwell on what would happen. Could Jan be right? Did she and Reid share a bond? It would explain so much.

Tammy would have never thought of herself as a love-at-first-sight girl, and yet from the moment she'd met the man, she could think of little else. Hell, even the fact that he turned into a ginormous bear didn't curtail the attraction or interest. If that didn't scream true lov—

A sharp *pop* sent the SUV careening wildly. On the edge of a steep embankment, the front tire got caught by the edge, and next thing Tammy knew, they were whipping down it.

Tammy hollered, "Ohmyfuckinggod."

Jan cursed just as vividly as she fought the wheel and pumped the brakes. Neither tactic slowed their frightening descent, nor did it move the trees fast approaching.

With a warning of "brace yourself!" they hit. Air bags, impact, and a bonked head, though, meant Tammy missed what happened next.

Head throbbing, mind groggy, when Tammy next opened her eyes, it took her a moment to orient herself. Last thing she remembered, she and Jan were heading for a tree. She even vaguely recalled the crunch of impact. *I survived.* And she was no longer in the truck.

She'd traded her front row seat for a prone one. Strapped to a gurney, an IV feeding into her arm, Tammy struggled to understand what was happening because, despite the tube and hospital type bed with its metal rails, she wasn't recovering in a medical facility. Not unless Alaska kept patients in metal hangars with high arched, ribbed ceilings where hanging fluorescent lights highlighted the fact several vehicles were parked alongside her. She was pretty sure even the most remote location would frown on that. So if she wasn't in a hospital, where was she?

"The human awakes. About time. I was beginning to think my little plan killed you." That didn't sound good. The mocking voice came from a spot to her left, and she tilted her head in an attempt to locate the speaker.

The bleak illumination helped her see that many men milled around, all warmly dressed, despite what appeared to be several propane heaters, their red elements glowing as tubing for ventilation ran from them. How reassuring. She wouldn't die of carbon monoxide poisoning, but given someone was pumping her veins full of some dark substance, she wouldn't count herself quite lucky yet.

"Who are you? Where am I?" she asked, her words sluggish and thick as she struggled to speak through the fog still permeating her thoughts and muscles.

"I am a ghost of the past, the scourge of the present and the new leader of the future," announced the large man. And she meant large. Sporting a military-short cut of shocking white hair, the massive fellow grinned at her, teeth white and straight, eyes a mismatched green and blue. A scar ran from his temple to his chin, an angry purple-red line that made his genial smile all the scarier.

Tammy tried to quell the fear icing her veins, or was it whatever they were injecting in her that caused the chilling sensation? "What do you want with me? And where's Jan?"

"The blonde? She's slipped our grasp for the moment. Wily creatures, those foxes. Never fear, though, I've got men looking for her."

Despite her predicament, Tammy offered up a quick prayer they wouldn't find Jan. At this point, Tammy didn't think an extra prayer for herself would do much good. The term 'royally fucked' came to mind.

"Why do you want her, and me for that matter? We've not done anything to you."

"No, you haven't, but you both have men who would die to see you again."

"You mean Reid?"

"Among others. Way I hear it, the Kodiak has become quite attached to his little human from the city. Why, there are rumors swirling he might even claim you."

"How can there be rumors? I've only been here a few days."

"This isn't the dark ages, dear girl. There is a thing called the internet and texting. Of course, the picture I posted of your last smooch with the bear didn't require any caption."

"You've been spying on us?"

"Spying. Observing. Tattle-telling. Or as I like to call it, stirring up trouble. As a shifter, who is of course concerned about the leadership in Kodiak Point, it was my duty to report the behavior of the clan's alpha. Basically his unseemly relationship with a human. It's got some of the other groups in quite the uproar. See, there's many a mama and a poppa hoping their little shifter darling would catch that big bear's eye. They aren't too happy Reid might spoil future generations by mixing his blood with a human."

"They don't have to worry. Reid's already made it clear that I have no place in his future."

"Giving up so easily?" The scary stranger's brows rose high with false incredulity. His feral smile widened. "We can't have that. I like it when the clans are grumbling. I like it when Reid is scrambling. I especially enjoy seeing him suffer."

"Why?" Tammy uttered the single word query automatically, hearing the anger in the white-haired man's tone while seeing the madness in his eyes.

"You don't really expect me to spill my secrets so soon and so easily, do you? Suffice it to say that I've got a plan. A many tiered one to bring him down while I watch and cheer."

"If you hate him so much, why play games? Why not confront him?"

"A fight is too easy. Too quick. I need Reid to suffer. I want him to watch, helpless, as everything he loves crumbles around him."

"You're nuts."

"Crazy? Me?" He laughed, a chilling sound, colder than the cavernous room around them. "Most assuredly and it's all his fault. Him and his cronies. Never fear, I have plans for them too."

"I still don't understand what this has to do with me. Like I said, Reid and I might have hooked up a few times, but it never went any further. I was on my way back home."

"In the wrong direction. Or did you think I didn't notice your turning around? You should have kept going. I was thinking of letting you go and just going after the fox, but the opportunity was just too good."

"You orchestrated our accident?"

"Just call me maestro."

A sharp cramp went through her, a slicing agony that forced a gasp from her lips.

The man's eyes narrowed and his lips thinned into a tight smile. "I see you're starting to feel the effects."

"What are you doing to me?" Tammy pulled at the straps binding her to the bed. The leather cuffs didn't loosen one bit, but the cramping in her body increased.

"Doing? Why, what your beloved Kodiak would never do. What most shifters fear to do because the mortality rate is so high. I'm giving you a chance to become one of us."

"Why would you want that?"

"Because if you survive, and I return you to him, then every time he looks at you, I want him to think of me. To know a part of me runs in your veins."

"You're giving me blood?"

"Blood and what makes me special."

"What do you mean?"

"Did your precious bear not explain the possibility? Not all shifters are born. Some are created. All it takes is blood, a lot of it, and a strong specimen. You should thank me for granting you this gift. As a human, you are frankly, quite unsuitable for an alpha leader. But as one of us..." He smiled wide, his pointed canines glinting. "As one of us, there is no reason you should be apart. If you survive the change that is, which according to the latest statistics compiled, is one out of every thirteen."

"But I don't want to be a shifter."

"Then maybe you'll be one of the dozen who die."

Before she could argue that choice, pain swept through her, stealing her breath and her voice. It stole everything from her, including all thoughts but one.

Someone help me.

Chapter Twenty-four

It took Reid a moment to breathe and think coherently when he caught up to Boris and the site of the crashed SUV; crumpled metal, deflated airbags, the strong stench of wolf, bear, fox, and a myriad other creatures. Some of the scents came from his own clan members who combed the wreckage and nearby wooded ravine, their paws and, in some cases, still-human steps marring the pristine whiteness of the snow. Other odors, though, he didn't recognize.

Traces of blood, a familiar metallic scent, made him growl as his bear reacted to the violence, a growl that turned into a roar as he noted the blown-out tire.

This was no accident.

"Where are the women?" he shouted, seething with anger—but also cold with fear because it didn't take much to connect the dots. Someone had shot at Jan's truck, sent it, along with its occupants, careening off the road, and then ... what? Absconded with Jan and his city girl? Killed them?

Another roar erupted, and those around him spared him a wary glance, but none dared speak to him. None but Boris. The big man approached, implacable as ever. Did nothing ever shake the rugged moose?

Or was the stony façade just a front? Reid noted Boris' clenched fists, and the dark ice in his eyes. Only someone close to him, someone like Reid, who'd been through hell and back with the man, would recognize the signs of the moose teetering on the edge of control. If Boris snapped … blood would flow.

"Are you done roaring?" Boris asked dryly.

"I'll roar if and when I damn well like," Reid snapped.

"What the fuck happened here?"

"Some idiots fucked with the wrong guys. They'll pay for what they've done," Boris said with grim promise.

Of course they'd pay. As if Reid would allow this type of attack to go unpunished. "Any clues on who did this? I want the one responsible so we can tear them limb from limb."

"All I can really tell you is this wasn't the work of one man. By my count as least six, possibly up to eight people, were involved. Four snowmobiles in total."

"Did they take the women with them?" Unvoiced was the true question: were they alive? "What about their trail? They must have left one since they came in on machines."

"If I'm reading the signs correctly, Jan shifted and took off on foot, but her trail gets murky at one point, not far from here. The other signs point to your woman being taken. As to her state of being…" Boris shrugged. "She's human. Fragile. Who knows if she survived the impact or not, although I would imagine they wouldn't bother to cart around a corpse."

Small consolation, but Reid would take it. *She's not dead. She can't be.* He'd know it if she were.

Feel it. Of that, he, and his bear, were certain. "What were you saying about Jan? How did she end up running from them?"

His stoic expression turned grim. "Her situation I'm less sure of. Looks like she flipped into her fox. I followed her tracks a distance, but her dad taught her well. I lost her trail."

If the situation weren't so dire, Reid might have laughed at Boris' dour statement. "Outfoxed by a woman, imagine that."

"Stubborn chit should have never been out here in the first place," Boris grumbled. "But no, you had to forbid the insurance broad from leaving, and Jan just had to flout the rules, as usual, and take matters into her own hands."

"Maybe if she had a man to keep her in line—" Reid caught the elbow before it jabbed him in the stomach. "Someone's testy. Got a problem with the idea of Jan pairing up with someone else?"

"Why would I care what that woman does? I was just testing your reflexes. You're going to need them if you're going after the human. At least I assume you're going after her?"

As if there was any doubt. "Fucking right I am. And am I correct in assuming that you'll be hunting down our resident fox?"

"Someone's got to get that girl out of trouble," Boris grumbled, but Reid could sense the man's anxiety. Much as Boris might grumble and grouse, he felt something for Jan. He just wouldn't admit it.

Kind of like Reid had refused to recognize what was right under his nose.

"How many men do you want with you?" Reid asked.

"None. They'll just get in my way. Besides, by the looks of it, you'll need them more than me."

Probably, if Boris' estimate was correct. Reid also had to figure that wherever they'd taken Tammy might also have more men. Possibly armed ones. He'd need all the warm bodies he could muster.

Guilt over sending Boris off alone without backup never crossed his mind. If anyone was capable of taking care of his own ass and tracking a fox who'd gone into hiding, then it was the man who'd emerged from a nasty war and made it home more or less in one piece. Although, Brody often teased him about having left his sense of humor, along with his girly locks, behind. The short buzz cut was definitely a far cry from Boris' rocker-long hair of his teens.

"Good luck," Reid said, slapping the moose on the back. "And keep in touch."

Boris just grunted in reply as he straddled his snowmobile and gunned off, a man on a mission, one Reid could almost pity. If Boris did find Jan, the only thing he probably needed to fear was a woman scorned and himself. Boris became his own worst enemy when it came to a certain blonde.

As the rumble of his engine faded, Reid readied himself for departure. He stuck a few fingers in his mouth and blew. His strident whistle brought his clansmen, some shifted, others not, to gather around.

He didn't waste time launching into a speech. Simple was best. "Follow the tracks to the bastards who did this. And then, tear them apart." Forget fancy words or mercy.

You touched what was mine. Now you die.

Whoever caused the crash hadn't felt a strong need to cover their tracks. Almost as if they wanted to be found. Lucky in one respect, as it meant he and his guys could make good time following on their sleds, but worrisome as it meant he probably headed into a trap.

He didn't care. Tammy still lived. His enemy had her. By the rules of any game, it meant he had to go, fight, and end, once and for all, the deadly games his invisible opponent wanted to play.

They rode for less than two hours before they came across signs of civilization. Not civilization in the form of houses and stores, but tamped trails, a myriad of scents, and smoke drifting on a light breeze.

They ditched their snowmobiles and, in some of his men's cases, their clothes as they headed the rest of the way on foot.

Nothing but the soft crunch of snow and ice marred the quiet serenity of the early dark. As for their goal, it loomed ahead of them, a metal hangar, ribbed and windowless. Around it was scattered smaller buildings, sheds really. While the ground bore signs of recent vehicular activity, not a truck or car or anything was parked in sight.

But Reid wasn't fooled by the seemingly abandoned nature of the place. He didn't need his bear's agitated pacing inside his mind to sense the danger. Menace existed and watched. The hairs on his body, even under the many layers, tingled as he felt eyes on him.

Not one to sneak like a coward, Reid halted and planted his hands on his hips. He bellowed, "Come out, you fucking pansy-assed coward, and fight me."

He didn't expect his faceless adversary would, but to his surprise, a mocking answer arrived. A gravelly voice said, "Look who's calling me a coward. How ironic. Let's see just how brave you are. Why don't you come inside? I've got a *warm* welcome for you."

Oh, how cliché and ridiculously super villainous. Reid laughed. "That is the worst line I've ever heard. Let me give you a better one. Let's end this. Right here, right now. Man to man. Or bear to whatever you are."

"A fight? As if a fight ever truly solves anything."

Whatever happened to the good old days where disputes were solved with fists and then laughed about over a few beers? Some days Reid missed his time in the military. Especially the brave men he encountered and served with. Courageous men, unlike the one he currently dealt with. A true opponent wouldn't hide. "I've got better things to do than waste my time with a coward."

"Coward? That's rich coming from you."

"Says the guy who won't show his face. Are you going to come out and face me or not?"

"What if I say no? What will you do, *bear*?"

"Proclaim far and wide that the man who thought to usurp my spot didn't have the balls to face me."

"So you'd leave? What a shame. And here I had a surprise waiting for you. Won't she be disappointed? Ah well. I guess I misjudged your interest in her. I can't say as I blame you. Humans are so delicate, and a man in your position can't afford weakness."

Those words got his attention. "What have you done to Tammy? Where is she?"

A low chuckle rolled out of a speaker that Reid finally located strung above the only door into the hangar. "You want the woman? Then come and get her."

Yes, it was a trap. And, yes, it was a bad idea. It didn't stop Reid. Not once he knew his city girl was inside.

Signaling to Travis and some of the others to circle around to the back of the hangar, he sprinted with a few more of his clan to the door, which swung open at his approach.

Not a good sign. "Du—"

The first shot cracked, whizzed by him so close he felt the zing of its passing. It hit too. Just not him. With a yelp, one of his guys hit the ground with a thump and cursed, "They're using fucking silver. Bastards."

The ultimate betrayal when it came to turf wars between clans or rogues looking to stake a claim. The unspoken unwritten rules of the shifter clans stated no outside weapons. Most especially not silver, the bane of their existence. A metal the hunters of old used on them. Or so his grandfather claimed.

Despite the close encounter with mortality, Reid didn't slow his approach. However, he did watch the opening more closely. When he saw the barrel poking out again, he yelled, "Incoming."

Their military training, and his tone of command, meant they obeyed without question. Bodies hit the ground, and the shot whistled harmlessly overhead.

There was no third attempt as the gravelly-voiced fellow shouted through the screaming feedback on the speaker, "You fucking idiot. I told you I wanted the bear alive."

Great. Because alive, Reid could cause so much more damage.

And carnage.

He dove through the open portal, rolled, and popped to his feet, quickly scanning the environ. He managed a mental snapshot of the moment and interior.

Not exactly the most encouraging of places. Neglect hung over the abandoned hangar. The remnants of vehicle parts and machinery littered the floor and clustered along the wall. The concrete floor, what was visible, bore the dust of abandonment and detritus of animals claiming the space. Yet amidst the signs of neglect were those of more recent inhabitants. A pile of garbage, its reek held at bay by the radiating cold, which the scattered propane heaters couldn't quite keep at bay. Ratty old mattresses also lay scattered here and there, sleeping bags strewn across them, a makeshift camp of vermin Reid planned to eradicate.

All these details he absorbed within a moment. However, most of it got shoved away in the later file. The most pressing issue, in his mind at any rate, was about twenty feet away from him. A gurney with a prone figure atop it, covered to the chin in a sheet. The face angled away from him. But he could guess the identity given the curls and the glimpse of red the person wore.

Before he could take a step, someone tossed a fire-lit rag on the floor. With a *whoosh*, a ring of fire rose like a curtain around the bed with the body.

His city girl lay helpless in the midst of the fiery circle. "What the fuck have you done?" he queried, more than a little taken aback at the craziness of the moment. Fire, the second thing shifters didn't mess with. The forest was their friend. Fire annihilated it. Hence, they had a healthy respect for the most dangerous of elements.

"Choices, choices," a voice mocked, the speaker hidden by the haze of smoke. "Save the girl. Find me. Or save yourself. What will you do, *soldier*?"

The way he said it … the mocking tone. It seemed somehow familiar. Another clan traitor like the drivers? Did it matter? By betraying him, they forfeited their lives. Later. Right now he needed to deal with dancing flames that perfumed the space with toxic smoke. "Why make a choice? How about I do it all?" Starting with the most pressing concern. Tammy.

Already the heat and smoke were proving uncomfortable, and if he found it so with his strength and training, then how must it feel to his fragile city girl? Prone on the gurney, she'd yet to move, something that worried him but shoved to the back of his mind lest it distract him. He needed to get to her, but how? The fire would singe him. Moisture would help, but he had no access to running water and didn't spot an extinguisher.

Only old machine parts, wooden pallets on the inside, and snow on the outside. Snow. Wait a second, snow was—

Yeah, the light bulb went off, and it took only an instant to shed his clothes so he could shift. As he lumbered back outside, he tried to ignore the taunting voice. "Running away? So soon? If only your clan could see their fearless leader now."

If only they could. They'd wonder why his giant bear ass was making the biggest Kodiak snow angel ever seen.

Snow coating his fur in thick clumps, Reid ran back in, four legs pumping, straight toward the fire. The icy particles caught in his fur melted at the heat, but he didn't sizzle or burn. Much. The soles of his paws did get uncomfortably warm, but nothing he couldn't handle.

But how long would his luck hold? And now that he'd breached the ring, how would he get Tammy out? It wasn't as if he could roll her in a snowbank. A problem to worry about once he'd freed her.

With sharp teeth, he grasped at the leather straps holding her, tearing them from her feverish limbs, while trying to ignore the possible damage he caused in doing so. A few bruises and abrasions on her skin were minor compared to the possibility of burning alive.

She opened her eyes as he tore the fourth cuff, eyes that seemed to have difficulty focusing. "Reid," she whispered. "Is that you?"

As his bear, he couldn't answer, but he did his best to nod.

Her eyes widened. Not in fear, but surprised shock. She croaked, "Behind—"

He whirled before she could finish and narrowly missed the swipe from a massive paw. If Kodiaks were king when it came to size, polar bears were emperors.

And, in this case, supposedly dead.

Gene?

Before Reid could truly process the fact a man he'd once called friend, thought lost long ago in a far away land, faced him, he was in a fight for his life.

When humans fought, there was a certain elegance to it, a dance where blows were exchanged, where speed and skill played a large part. In a duel between deadly predators, those things applied, but add in biting and clawing, and things got ugly, as well as bloody, real fast.

They also got very physical, and as the inferno raged around them, encircling them in a cage fire, Reid knew he fought for his life—and Tammy's. But Tammy wouldn't last long, not if his gasping for oxygen was any indication as the flames sucked at the air, making it hard to breathe.

Head-butting his opponent, Reid wrenched free and partially turned, enough that he could shove at the gurney holding Tammy. It shot like a rocket toward the wall of flame. He could only hope the fire wall's diminishing height meant the flames were weakening in strength.

A head butt into his side sent him staggering, and Reid didn't have time to watch and see if she made it safely. Once again, wrestling for his life, he could only hope if the inferno touched her that she would rouse enough to save herself. He'd done what he could to give her a chance. Now it was time to save himself from a ghost returned to haunt him.

And apparently kill me.

Chapter Twenty-five

An eternity of pain later, Tammy surfaced back into the world, unsure of anything other than the fact every part of her hurt. What the hell!

It was like having a full-body bruise. Every single part of her ached, and she whimpered. Prayed for some heavy-duty drugs. Even a warm—or gruff—voice to tell her everything would be all right.

She got squat. Much like that stupid tree in the forest, nobody seemed to hear. *Where's some attention when you need it?* Then again, it wasn't as if a soothing voice would have helped. *No, but even a couple acetaminophen would.* Oh, what she wouldn't give for a great big joint right about now. For its medicinal value of course.

She couldn't have said how long she floated on a wave of pain. If she had to guess, she would have said a long while, mostly because of the incomprehensible murmurs that encircled her. Too apathetic to care what they spoke of, she could only stew in her own misery.

And it's all my fault. Like a dumb ninny in a movie, she'd gone rushing off without a proper plan, a disregard for danger, letting her emotions rule instead of common sense. For that, she deserved a bitch slap. Not this. The memory of an IV dripping poison into her arm, faint-inducing agony, and a certainty this just wouldn't end well.

Speaking of ending, though, to her surprise, when the pain finally ebbed into numbness, she didn't immediately notice it. The gradual ease of tension and aches permeating her occurred so slowly and smoothly, she never took note. But when she did, a heavy sigh burst free. *Maybe I'm not going to have to worry about winning a TSTL Darwin-type award.*

The problem with sighing was it garnered her some attention. Ah, for the good old days, when she was easily ignored. Until she did something off the wall. Tammy never did like fading into the background.

A much-too-jovial voice, belonging to the guy with messed-up eyes, noted her consciousness. "She awakes! And just in time too. Your teddy bear is racing to your rescue."

Tammy had no problem deciphering his words. *Reid's coming to rescue me!*

She might have exulted in the news more if her skin didn't start itching worse than the time she'd rolled into a patch of poison ivy. Multiply the I-need-to-scratch-NOW feeling by ten and you might have understood her newest torture. Worse, she couldn't move to ease it, not with the straps binding her to the gurney. A lack of mobility, of course, made the itch worse.

Everything irritated her from the leather chafing her exposed wrists and ankles to the bright lights above. Those pupil-seeking bastards seemed determined to burn holes through her eyelids. Her sympathy for mythical vampire figures and their aversion to daylight, shifted. No more would she mock the nocturnally challenged.

A sharp crack of a gunshot made her moan as the sound reverberated in her head. *Hello, still in need of a pain reliever here.*

The second ringing bang didn't see her faring any better. She struggled to open her eyes, utter a sound or move, but it was as if her body were apart from her, tethered to her consciousness yet adrift when it came to use. Probably not a bad thing considering her untenable situation.

A situation that was about to get better?

She heard the rumble of an animal, a bear. How she knew, she couldn't have said. But something within her recognized it.

Consciousness wavered for a moment as she struggled and strained to understand what happened. This whole unable-to-see-events-unfolding sucked. Relying on her other senses made her feel so vulnerable and out of the loop. Deciphering the situation was like putting together puzzle pieces blind. She did her best though.

It seemed those torturing her were under attack. Good news for her, but luck short-lived as she heard a *whoosh* that sent a chill through her.

Oh no. Not again.

Those who've lived through certain traumas remember key aspects. For victims of tornados, it was seeing that cone of wind and debris. For Tammy, her trigger was that whooshing noise, the sound fire made when it announced its grand entrance, hungry and ready to consume everything in its path. *And crisp my chubby thighs into Tammy bacon. Everyone knows everything's better with bacon.*

Humor didn't alleviate her terror. Smoke tickled her sensitive nasal passages, its invasive stench permeating the air and bringing forth a whimper. Memories long forgotten, memories she'd buried and locked away for her own peace of mind, surfaced and forced her to recall the last time she'd confronted fire.

Just a child, she'd gone to the cabin with her dad. A father-daughter weekend of target shooting and fishing. Of roasting marshmallows and snuggling as he read her a book.

A crisp and cool night, her father built her a crackling fire. They were just about to read some fairy tale with a dragon and his princess when it happened. A simple everyday occurrence, a popping ember from the fireplace. A hot glowing chunk hit the rug and didn't immediately extinguish.

Her father, barefoot at the time and thus unable to stamp it out, urged her to fetch a glass of water. Tammy rushed to the sink and the counter with its keg of water. No well meant they brought their water with them in big plastic jugs with a tap in the side. A tap that poured molasses slow.

Young and clumsy, she tripped and spilled the cupful of liquid before she could return. By the time she'd fetched another, curling smoke rose from a dancing flame.

"Run outside, Tammy. Let me take care of this, and then you can come back in for a story," her father urged as he grabbed the small cup of liquid and splashed it. She would always remember the sizzling sound of her tiny cup of water as he poured it over the growing fire, a sound that said not enough. But she'd not understood at the time. She'd skipped outside, convinced her daddy would fix it. Daddy fixed everything.

But her daddy didn't count on the speed with which a hungry fire could spread, especially since he never noticed the second chunk of ember that also spat forth. From the overheard hushed whispers she gleaned in the aftermath, he'd gone to fill a bigger jug at the kitchen counter while the second unnoticed coal burned. He should have followed his advice to his daughter and left while he could. As the slow flowing tap on the jug filled the container, the flames from both spots multiplied, quickly cutting off his only exit.

Tammy could still hear his screams chasing her as she ran through the woods in her bare feet, running for help. Help that was already too late.

It took her years of nightmares, therapy, and cheesecake-flavored ice cream before she overcame her panic attacks and terror each time she caught a flicker. Especially embarrassing when she had a meltdown moment in a big department store over the fake fire in one of their floor display fireplaces.

Nothing like having a classmate witness an ignoble panic attack for her to decide she wouldn't let the past destroy her. It took time, but she eventually vanquished the nightmares. Learned to master fire and savor the taste of a barbecued steak. Heck, she even returned to the place where she'd shared so many wonderful memories with her father. But she'd never quite shaken free the guilt—and the terror—fire invoked.

As the smoke grew thicker and the temperature rose, she forced open her eyes in time to see Reid as he tore through the last of her restraints. At least she assumed it was him. Big, shaggy bear sporting an intent expression and an ornery snarl.

So adorable, if scarily impressive.

She whispered his name and would have said more, like, "Hey, thanks for coming." She really was more grateful than he could imagine. However, fate was really having a bitchin' day with her. As if Tammy hadn't gone through enough, now her unlikely rescue was getting screwed with.

Why can't anything go right?

Over Reid's shoulder loomed a massive white bear. If Reid was tall, this beast was beyond ginormous. He towered behind Reid, and given she recognized the mismatched eyes of her abductor, she doubted he wished her big bear well. She opened her mouth to shout. Nothing but a hoarse "behind" emerged, and yet Reid understood—and pulled a total bonehead guy move.

He ignored his own safety and took care of her.

Adorable idiot.

As Reid shoved her wheeled bed at the ring of flames, the oxygen-hungry fire stole what breath she had to scream.

Crazy fucking b—

A curse unfinished as a terrified moan seeped from her, screams echoing in her mind as flames threatened to devour her. The heat seared her exposed skin, but worse, some of it latched on to the bedding she lay upon. For a moment, she stared in paralyzed horror at the pretty orange and yellow flicker dancing on the edge of the bed. *Hello,* it seemed to say. *Remember me?*

Yes. Yes, she did. Murdering bastard.

With a cry of rage or fear or something wholly inexplicable, Tammy threw herself from the gurney, her muscles not entirely co-operating. She ended up in a crumpled heap on the concrete floor.

Ow!

Not her most delicate of landings, but at least the fire hadn't won. Yet. She could still hear it mocking as it sizzled and popped. Where was a fireman when she needed one?

Of more concern, while she had emerged mostly unscathed from the arena constructed of gasoline and flame, Reid remained within it, his large furry shape currently wrestling with a massive polar bear.

Welcome to the most extreme animal documentary ever. When a Kodiak bear confronts an arctic terror, who will survive within the burning ring of fire? And why did she fight a hysterical giggle as she suddenly thought of a commercial for diarrhea?

Reid reeled from a savage blow, and all mirth dissipated. As control of her limbs returned, she edged closer to the flames. Hypnotized. With streaming eyes and burning lungs, Tammy couldn't help her riveted stare as the massive beasts fought. Odd how a part of her wished she could join in.

Given blood coated them both, and neither seemed to show signs of slowing down, she couldn't really tell who held the upper hand. The pure savagery did stun her, though.

It was hard to remember that somewhere amidst the fur and muscles, were men. But in such an epic battle, only one could survive. The massive polar took a huge gash to his side, and crimson flowed, the color stark against its white fur.

With a roar of agony, and a cringe by Tammy, the polar bear shrank and contorted until only a man lay panting on the floor. She couldn't quite hear the words he said, but she saw Reid's face, his human face as he also changed and loomed over his fallen foe. Reid appeared ... sad?

He held out a hand, as if to help the white-haired guy up, a guy who only moments ago had tried to kill him. Tammy screamed a warning as she saw her abductor grasp at something and raise his hand. The cheater had a pistol!

"Watch o—"

Too late. Again. She really needed to work on spitting out her warnings quicker. A sob left her as Reid peered down at his chest, incredulous. His eyes met hers, and he mouthed, "Run."

But she couldn't. Even as he fell to a knee and the curtain of flames screened him mostly from her view. Mostly. She still saw him topple over. Dead. Gone.

She uttered a harsh wail then a sharp scream as the next bullet her kidnapper fired nicked her upper bicep. Everything inside her exploded in that moment. Anger annihilated her fear. Adrenaline fueled the unco-operative muscles in her body. "You fucking jerk. What is wrong with you?" Furious suddenly at herself, the world, and especially the asshole who'd caused all the current drama, she leaned down and grabbed something heavy.

In Tammy's youth, her mother thought the time she'd spent tossing the ball with her dad such a waste. *"Why play boys' sports when we could be painting our nails together? Or shopping?"* her mother would say.

Because one day, knowing how to throw something and hitting a target might come in handy. Like right about now. She lobbed the chunk of metal from some abandoned machine at her abductor's head.

Her aim was off, but finally her luck turned. She hit the gun and uttered a satisfied noise as it spun out of the polar guy's hand. *That'll work.*

It didn't seem to bother him. With a wave at her and a grin—which really needed a good slap—her tormentor took off running in the opposite direction, leaving her alone, trembling and sweating from the fire still ringing Reid's poor body.

His poor not dead body.

She saw Reid roll away from the flames, placing himself in the center, safe for the moment. However, even as the flames died down, the concrete unable to fuel it now that the gasoline and nearby debris was consumed, she knew Reid bled. *I can smell it.* Why or how was too icky to figure out. She needed to get to him and apply pressure on his wound until help arrived.

But how to get through the flames? *I need a hose. Water. Something.*

Not for the first time, she wished she had the equipment to extinguish a fire. While she had a full bladder, her aim was anything but accurate. So what else could she use to douse?

A chill breeze whipped through a banging door to the outside.

Of course. Snow. Rushing to the outside, she only vaguely noted the snarls and yelps as animals fought their own war of supremacy. For her, there was only one battle that counted—the one to keep Reid alive so she could berate him for being a dumbass.

How dare he charge to her rescue and put himself in harm's way, ensuring her safety then staying behind to fight, covering her retreat? That stupid, selfless jerk.

The tears streamed in steady rivulets, not enough to put out flames, but they probably didn't hurt the armfuls of snow she dumped on the fire. The shoveled ice chunks by the door were especially effective, as their ice-block texture kept the flames from turning them into steam. It took only three running trips back and forth for her to clear a path to Reid. She darted into the ring and dropped to her knees beside him.

Streaks of blood marred his skin, making it hard for her to find his bullet wound. Gentle swipes helped her locate the neat, round hole in his chest, which oozed only sluggishly.

Oh no. She was too late. He'd bled out!

"No, no, no," she muttered. He couldn't die. She pressed against the hole with her bare hand. Such heat radiated from him, as well as the steady beat of his heart, a cruel mockery as he lay on the threshold of death.

"You big idiot," she sobbed. "Why did you have to do that? I would have found a way to save myself." Or at least not be responsible for yet another death. Was she destined to forever lose men she loved to fire and impotence? Twice now, she'd gotten thrust to safety. Twice now, people she cared about had died because of her.

"Don't cry, city girl," said a raspy voice.

Swallowing sniffles, she peered into Reid's face to see his eyes open at half-mast. "Don't talk. Try and keep your strength. I don't know how, but I'll figure a way out of here." She'd fought past her fear of fire, and won. Surely she could prevail over death too?

"Don't leave," he whispered.

"Of course not. I'll never leave you."

"Ever?" he asked. "For as long as we both shall live?"

Such eerie words. Did he know the end had arrived? She promised. "Never. I'll be at your side until your last breath."

The sudden smile of triumph didn't clue her in, but when Reid rolled her under his body and pinned her, she figured it out.

"You're not dying," she stated.

"Nope."

"You asshole," she yelled, pushing at him. As if she could budge a mountain. "Let me go."

"Hey, what happened to never leaving my side?"

"I only said that because I thought you were dying."

"Still counts."

"Does not," she snapped.

"Whatever. I'm holding you to it."

Dirty, annoyed, and heart still pounding with adrenaline didn't mean she didn't find his determination to keep her hot. Yes, he'd fooled her, with the intent purpose of getting her to agree to stay. Total turn-on. "Don't you have something better to do right now, like chase after that polar bear dude or find that toilet paper your kind are so fond of?"

She loved how his lips turned into a grin. "Only the softest for my sweet cheeks. And as for Gene, didn't you hear the helicopter blades? He's long gone, so no point in aggravating my bullet wound. I might heal quicker than a full-blooded human, but I still shouldn't overdo it. Besides, I like where I am."

Considering their position—him atop her, fully naked, and distinctly aroused, yeah, he *really* liked his spot. Still, though, now was not the time. "Did you say a helicopter? What the hell, Reid? I feel like I'm living a part in a very corny, mobster-type movie, and I don't like it at all."

"Not mobster, shifter. And believe it or not, life isn't usually this fucked up."

"Then what is it usually?"

"It was boring. Dull. Lonely."

"Gee, that sounds like fun." She wrinkled her nose.

He rubbed his nose against hers, a gentle and intimate gesture she wouldn't have expected from him. "You missed the *was* part. That all changed when a pan-wielding city girl with a mean aim entered my life."

"Can I help it if you bring out the best in me?" She couldn't help but smirk.

He laughed. "And there you go again, making me happy. It's so annoying."

"Excuse me."

"In a good way," he amended. "I'd forgotten what it was like to feel actual happiness. To truly laugh. I also like that you're not afraid of me and can stand toe to toe with me."

"As if I'd let a bear order me around."

"Just don't misbehave in public. I do have an image to maintain."

"Is that a challenge?"

He growled.

She laughed.

"Good thing I know we're meant to be together, or I'd wonder if you were sent to punish me."

She groaned. "You did not just say that. What is it with you shifter types? Jan had some messed-up theory about us being fated mates."

"Not theory. Fact. You're *mine*."

Possessive to the extreme, and the most arousing moment of her life. Still, though, could she believe him? "I thought you were all bound and determined to sacrifice your virtue to the clan with the most well-connected daughter."

"That was before you went missing."

"That bothered you?" She almost held her breath waiting for his answer.

"Are you trying to force me to tell you that I lost my bear-loving mind? I did. In that moment, I realized that once I found you—"

"Because you were so sure you would."

"As if there was any doubt."

"So cocky." And hot.

"I thought I told you before, it's assertive."

"Whatever. So what did you realize?"

"I could never let you go."

Puddle of goo inside her chest? Yeah, that was her melted heart. "What about your clan?"

"What about them? I'm the alpha and a Kodiak fucking bear. It occurred to me I could do whatever the hell I liked and, if they didn't like it, too fucking bad."

God, it was sexy when he got all bad-ass I-am-the-boss. "And what is it you want to do?"

"Isn't it obvious?" He tossed her a grin that stole whatever breath she had to reply. His head lowered until he could whisper against her lips. "I want to do you."

Chapter Twenty-six

The problem with romantic declarations while covered in blood, still injured, and out in the open on a battlefield was you could almost guarantee an interruption. This time it came in the shape of Travis, an automatic rifle over one shoulder, a bandana around his forehead, and not a stich of clothing. To Reid's amusement, and as a balm to his jealousy, Tammy immediately turned her head.

Travis would live another day.

"Boss, you're alive, and I see you found your lady."

"I did," Reid said. He couldn't help a spurt of pleasure despite the throb of pain in his chest. Death wouldn't claim him this day, but he on the other hand would claim his city girl. A city girl who'd risked herself to save him. A city girl he'd tricked into promising to stay. *My city girl. Mine.*

With the adrenaline of battle still warming his blood, there were other things Reid would have preferred to do than speak with his cousin. However, now wasn't the time or place to indulge in selfish desires. Tammy had fared well to this point, but she was human. She'd gone through a traumatic experience. He needed to get her out of here and somewhere safe, with a shower—and a bed.

Holding back a sigh and with only a slight wince, Reid got to his feet. He held out a hand to

Tammy, whose cheeks flushed red, noticeable even under the layer of soot. How cute that nudity still embarrassed her. Shifters never suffered from that minor quirk. "What can you report?" Reid asked his cousin as he draped an arm around her.

"We've got a bunch of the rogue shifters on the run. Those that got ditched at any rate. Did you know they had a fucking helicopter stashed under a tarp outside?"

"I heard it. Could you tell who was aboard?"

"A couple of guys, one of them some white-haired dude, who waved. Cocky fellow. I take it he was the one who set this trap and took your girl?"

"Yes." Reid kept his answer short. While Travis had heard of Gene, he'd never met him. How could he? Dead men usually didn't visit. Until now.

It still blew Reid away once he'd realized who he faced. They'd exchanged a few words, mostly incredulous ones.

"Holy fuck, Gene, you're alive."

"Surprise. Bet you never expected to see me again."

No, because the last time Reid saw him, the rebel soldiers were dragging Gene away to their special place. The place all of them were taken for special attention as the enemy sought to get them to spill their secrets. Gene never returned, and when Reid and the others escaped, they'd assumed him dead. Wrong.

"It was real nice of you to make an effort to free me," Gene said as he lay on the ground bleeding from the gash in his side.

"If we'd have known—"

"You'd have what? Risked your life and chance to escape on me?" Gene chuckled, a rattly sound. "Liar."

The gunshot took him by surprise. Why did his old military friend try to kill him? Did he honestly blame Reid for not coming to his rescue? Then again, Gene wouldn't be the first soldier to survive a trauma and blame others for his ordeal.

Question was, what was Gene's ultimate plan?

Reid wasn't stupid. Gene could have killed him well before the fight. He had the men and the manpower. But instead, he'd fought Reid. It was almost as if he wanted to … play?

Surely not, and yet, Reid couldn't shake the sense that Gene wasn't after Reid's death so much as he wanted him to suffer. If he looked at the series of events leading to this confrontation, it all added up to annoyances and nips at Reid's power. Jabs at him. A vengeful torture for an imagined slight?

Yet it wasn't my fault he got caught that day. We were all so unprepared for what happened. Facts on his side or not, Reid couldn't deny this bore the marks of a plan from a deranged mind. Not his fault entirely, and yet while he felt sorry for Gene, he wouldn't allow it to stop him from doing what he had to in order to protect his clan.

And keep my city girl safe.

Chapter Twenty-seven

By no means would Tammy consider herself a prude, and she definitely had a healthy appreciation for the male body—especially well-built naked ones. That didn't stop her, though, from blushing beet red as a very bare-assed Reid held a conversation with a very bare-assed Travis. Not just Travis though. Reid seemed determined to conduct a "hey, what's going on?" dialogue with every naked, bare-assed man he came across.

At one point, with so many appendages waving around, it was hard to find something to stare at, not because the sight of so much equipment aroused her. Only Reid himself could make her heart race faster. It was just, dammit—

"Could you all put some clothes on?" she finally shouted. "Like really, I understand you're shapeshifters and all, but I mean come on, it is freaking minus a zillion outside, and I'm really concerned that certain parts of you will freeze and fall off."

She probably deserved the laughter, but the kiss Reid planted on her lips, in full sight, and not of the chaste variety, stole her wits and any retort.

When he finally allowed her to breathe again, he murmured against her lips, "With remarks like that, is it any wonder I want you? All of you, fearless comments and all."

"There's a lot of me to want, and I don't just mean my attitude." Fishing for a compliment and reassurance? Given her past history, damned straight.

"I'm a man who likes curves," he growled against her ear before nipping the lobe with his teeth. Mmm, she felt that jolt right down to her toes. Where were a bed and some privacy when you needed them?

As clothing got tossed around, and the amount of bare skin—and animals wearing fur—disappeared, she caught more than one murmur mentioning the same name over and over again.

But given the commotion, she held her tongue. Some of the men got dressed, straddled their sleds and headed back for town, while others stayed behind to comb for clues and to keep an eye open for Boris, who searched for Jan. Reid was in the group who headed back home, Tammy clinging to his waist. Questions brimmed on the tip of her tongue, however a conversation at break-neck speed in the dark on the back of a snowmobile just wasn't feasible.

Her silence lasted only until they tumbled in from the cold into his kitchen. Of course, wouldn't it figure the chubby girl's first words would be, "I'm starved. Got anything we can eat in that giant fridge of yours?"

Her ex-boyfriend would have totally made her pay for her honest remark, something along the lines of "Geez, Tammy, can't you ever think of anything but food?"

Not when her tummy was grumbling.

Reid, though, was a whole different breed of man. Bear. Whatever. He grinned. "Have I told you I love the way you think? I'm sure we can find something. I can't have you fainting from hunger, not with what I have planned."

A plan to do what? It wasn't hard to guess by the wink he shot her and his sensual smile. As heat suffused her, she couldn't peel her winter layers fast enough. It didn't help the simmering fire within her but would make dessert a lot easier.

Reid made them both one of his massive sandwiches, which she inhaled, barely chewing. She could have eaten two. Who would have thought getting kidnapped and tortured would make a girl so hungry?

One need appeased, she addressed another one. Curiosity. "Who's Gene?"

In the process of placing their dirty dishes in the washer, Reid froze. "I don't suppose we could skip this conversation and leave it at 'someone from my past'."

"I kind of figured you knew each other. From where?"

"We served in the military and we used to be friends."

"What happened? Why does he have such a hate on for you?"

As he slammed the dishwasher door shut, Reid sighed. "My best guess? He thinks we intentionally abandoned him. We served in the same platoon together overseas. He was with me and a few others who were caught by rebel forces and held prisoner."

"Were you tortured?"

She didn't need his nod to read the bleak expression that crossed his face.

"But you escaped."

"We did, but Gene apparently didn't. We were separated, and when our chance came months later to get out, we didn't search for him because we thought he was dead. We guessed wrong."

"That's not your fault."

Reid rolled his shoulders. "Depends on your perspective, I guess. If I'd known Gene was still there, I would have turned the place upside down looking for him. But, given what he must have suffered, that's of little consolation. Apparently, now he's determined to make me pay."

"So what are you going to do?"

"What I have to," was Reid's grim reply.

Somehow Tammy didn't see a joyful reunion in the future. Not for a man who so callously toyed with other people's lives. "So he'll be back?"

"Probably. But now, at least we know who the enemy is. We can better prepare and erect defenses until he's caught."

"What does that mean for me?" Not an entirely selfish question given recent events. Tammy was all for women's lib and standing on her own two feet, but when it came to dealing with psychos, she wasn't too proud to lean on a man for help. If he was serious about wanting her.

"It means you'll have to be cautious, not go places by yourself for the moment and always carry a weapon."

"You talk as if I'm staying."

He arched a brow. "You are. I thought we clarified that back at the hangar."

"What if I'm not keen on living in a place where I'm constantly looking over my shoulder? What if I want to go home? Or—"

"And once again, you talk too much. I said you're staying, and that's final."

Another day or time, she might protest his heavy-handed attitude, but right now… The woman who'd always craved a man who could take control melted at his alpha declaration.

"You're bossy, Reid Carver."

"Yes."

"Overbearing."

"With good reason," he said with a grin.

"Really too cocky and sure of himself."

"I have to be."

"And sexy."

"Finally, she gives the bear a bone."

"I thought bears liked honey."

"This one prefers steak, and brown sugar. Not necessarily together, though."

"Now who's talking too much?" she grumbled.

He laughed as he reeled her into his arms. "I think I can fix that."

And he did by slanting his mouth over hers, an electric press of lips that made all her nerve endings come to life. Plus a few extra she'd never noted before.

Hunger, need, desire, they swirled within her making her frantic to have him.

"Impatient?" he growled against her ear as her hands tugged at the annoying fabric separating them.

"Sorry, I can't seem to stop myself," she replied, not sorry in the least as he obliged her by shedding his shirt and baring his chest. She ran her fingers over the hair dusting it. Tugged it. Let out a low growl when he grabbed at her hand and stopped her exploration.

"Let's move somewhere a little more comfortable and less likely to have an audience," he suggested.

A reasonable request, and yet a part of her, a primal corner she'd never noticed before, wanted to growl again at the delay. *Doesn't he understand I need him now?*

Her impatience must have shown because he tossed her over his shoulder, his big, brawny shoulder. As he jogged up the stairs, she had a lovely view of his taut backside flexing within his track pants. She grabbed at it and squeezed.

What I wouldn't give to bite it.

Another strange and stray thought, especially given Tammy wasn't the biting sort.

He bypassed the massive waiting bed and entered his large bathroom. "I think we could both use a shower," he explained.

Hot shower and a naked Reid? As if she'd argue. He set her on her feet then proceeded to strip her of her remaining clothes. Once she was naked, he stayed on his knees, nuzzling her round belly.

In the past, she might have found herself self-conscious. But with Reid so obviously enjoying her plentiful curves, who was she to ruin his fun? When he stood and palmed both her full cheeks with his hands, palpating them, she closed her eyes and couldn't help a smile when he said in a husky voice, "I love your ass. It is so fucking perfect."

"And fat."

"Yup, which is what I love most about it. Although I'll love it more when it's bent over for me and I get to slap up against it."

A crude compliment that meant more to her than any flowers. "So you really don't mind my extra pounds?" Again, she could have slapped herself for asking. But she'd been hurt so many times her ego could use the reassurance. And Reid gave it in spades.

"City girl, let me put this in words you might understand. I fucking love your body. Every curve. Every pound. Every silky inch. And before this night is through, I'm going to have licked, touched, and claimed all of it. More than once."

"Promise?" she asked with a smile as she draped her arms around his neck.

"Fucking right that's a promise," he growled as he walked them both into the piping hot shower.

The hot spray hit her back, and she angled her head to allow it to rinse her hair. She could almost feel the grime sluicing off her, a grime she'd barely noted when distracted by other events. She wasn't too distracted, though, to ignore Reid's hand. He'd grabbed some soap and ran it over her body, following her curves. Once again, he orated his liking of what he saw and felt.

"Mine." The possessive word wrapped her in a tingling vibration.

As he cupped her soapy breasts, his fingers rolled her nipples until they hardened into points.

She couldn't help the moan that slipped from her. It was only the first of many sounds as he tortured her breasts, teasing and pinching then turning her for a rinse so he could then latch onto her pert nubs with a hot mouth and grazing teeth.

Tammy squirmed and undulated with each sensuous touch, the heat suffusing her having nothing to do with the water of the shower. Reid was the one setting her on fire. Reid was the one making her pant. Moan. Tug at his hair. Beg.

"I need you," she said.

"Not yet," he replied.

She pouted. He laughed at her before spinning her to face the rear wall of his shower. Hands spread her cheeks, and hopeful he was done teasing, she arched her buttocks outward in open invitation.

He noticed, but instead of sliding his thick cock between her damp folds, his tongue swiped her.

Oh.

It lapped again. And again. He bathed her with his tongue then jabbed at her core with it. Hands braced against the wall, she keened her pleasure, loudly when his soft caresses moved from her sex to her clit. Her weak spot.

He flicked his tongue rapidly against her throbbing nub. Pleasure coiled within her, and her body tensed, tightened as it approached the edge of bliss. He didn't let up, but she tried to hold off coming. She wanted him inside her when she came. She wanted—

She screamed as he spoiled her plan with the thrust of his fingers into her clenching channel.

That combined with his tongue was too much. She orgasmed, big time.

But he wasn't done. His fingers pulled free of her throbbing sex but took the place of his tongue on her clit. He rubbed and rolled her nub as his thick cock head probed at her core.

Not quite over the ecstasy of her first orgasm, Tammy felt her second building. Then, and only then, did Reid allow himself to slide into her welcoming channel.

She couldn't help the convulsive squeeze as his thickness stretched her still-shuddering sex. He grunted. "So fucking tight and sweet."

"And about to come again if you don't hurry." She panted, unable to stop herself from rotating her hips to draw him deeper.

"Don't worry about me, city girl. I'm going to fuck you and claim you and make you scream when you come again."

And he did. He thrust into her, hard, fast strokes as his fingers pinched her clit. She screamed just as he predicted, and when he came, he fucking well roared.

It was the sexiest sound ever.

Chapter Twenty-eight

The next day, with Tammy safe at his aunt's house—along with his gun-toting ursa and a bevy of curious cousins—Reid called a clan meeting. He addressed several matters, first and foremost Gene's apparent vendetta against him and the town. Patrols were established, and the decision to send extra men in scout vehicles with truck shipments was made, an extra layer of protection until they caught the mad polar and his band of rabid friends and exterminated them.

As expected, the hot-blooded people he ruled approved of his no-mercy plan. But how would they react to his other news? Time to find out. He brought up the fact that he'd claimed Tammy. Less brought up than declared, "I've taken a human as my mate. If you don't like it, you can kiss my hairy ass."

Not surprising, no one decided to take him up on his offer. Actually, they seemed happy he'd decided to settle down.

"About time," someone shouted.

"She's cute," hollered another—a man Reid marked for a later talk. Just in case.

"Town could use some fresh blood."

Only one person dared mutter, "Thinking with his dick instead of the good of the clan."

But given one-hundred-and-three-year-old Jameson still believed woman shouldn't show their ankles in public, Reid didn't pay him much mind.

All in all, it went better than expected.

Not long after he adjourned the meeting and suffered the back slaps and commiserations from the men over getting shackled, his phone rang. It was Boris.

"I found her."

"Jan? She's okay?"

He heard a commotion and the murmur of arguing voices before Jan's smooth tone came on the line. "Of course, I'm fine. No thanks to big dumbass here, tromping around like, well, a big ol' moose and leading the enemy right to me."

"I took care of him," Boris said.

"With my help," she corrected.

"Taking down one wolf doesn't constitute help."

"It does if it's trying to chew your leg off," she retorted.

"You're trying my patience, woman," Boris grumbled in the background.

"I've already told you where to shove that. Would you like help?" Jan asked sweetly. "I assume that waggling finger means no? Then, in that case, if you don't mind, I'm talking to my boss. A civilized man. A man who isn't afraid to go after what he wants, unlike certain people."

"Are you calling me a coward?"

"Yes. I'm also willing to find some yellow paint and smear your belly with it."

"I am not afraid," he yelled.

Reid pulled the phone away from his ear and couldn't help casting it an incredulous glance as the pair continued to argue. Given they seemed to have forgotten him, and were obviously fine, he hung up. Maybe this incident would finally bring Boris around to the fact that he and Jan were meant to be together.

Highly unlikely. But then again, miracles could happen. Look at him and his city girl. Speaking of whom, he missed her already.

With his clan business more or less taken care of, or delegated, he hurried back to his aunt's house and walked in to an interesting scene.

His five cousins, ranging in age from mischievous to troublemaker, all stared at Tammy with wide eyes and open mouths.

They weren't the only ones sporting that expression. His city girl spun to face him and squeaked, "I roared at them."

"Can't say as I blame you. These rascals probably deserved it."

"No, you don't understand. I roared, as in like an animal roar."

Reid winced. Oops. He'd kind of hoped to address Tammy's *situation* before she noticed it. He gripped her by the arm and tugged her to the front hall, where he handed her clothing to layer on.

"What's going on, Reid?"

"We'll talk about it at my place," he said as he stalled. He pulled her from the house, practically shoving her into his still-warm truck.

"I don't want to wait, Reid. I want to know what's going on now!" Yeah, that last word came out with a bit of a grumbly, growly note.

He didn't reply as he backed out of the driveway and spun out onto the road.

"Reid? Why are avoiding my question?"

"We really should talk about this in private."

"I don't want to wait. I want to know what's happening now." When he didn't answer, she snarled, "Answer me, dammit." She slapped a hand over her mouth then squealed as she noted the claws on said hand.

Apparently this conversation wouldn't wait. Midway to his place, on a road bereft of houses, Reid pulled over and tried to find a way to tactfully explain. Fuck that.

"You're a shapeshifter."

He winced at her shrieked, "What?"

"I kind of suspected when I saw you strapped to the gurney, but I figured it out last night. Your, um, scent and extra vigor in bed kind of gave it away."

"You mean I stink? Of what? And how did this happen? I thought that couldn't happen with sex or a bite."

"It can't. But, in rare cases, sometimes a blood transfusion can change a human." He thought it wise not to mention at this point in time that she was lucky to be alive. And sane. Not everyone came through the procedure as well as she had.

"You mean Gene wasn't kidding when he claimed he was turning me into an animal?" Tammy slunk down in her seat with a moan. "Oh god. This is not happening."

"It's not that bad."

"Says you. You just told me I'm a shifter."

"Which, once you get the hang of it, is actually pretty cool."

"So what animal am I?"

"Judging by your scent? Bear. Polar I think."

"Ugh. You mean I'm like that Gene dude's mutant daughter now?"

Damn. She was. Crap. Would that change his plans to hunt his old friend? Probably not. Unlike vampires, she didn't need her maker alive to survive.

"It'll be fine. You'll probably have your first change during the full moon in about two weeks, and I'll be there every step of the way with you."

"I'll be fine?" She laughed, a touch of hysteria threading the sound. "I'm going to turn into a freaking polar bear on the next full moon, and you say everything is fine?"

"Of course it is because you're with me." *When rationalization fails, resort to alpha tendencies.* Oh, and kisses. He dragged her onto his lap, not exactly the most comfortable or amorous of spots given the steering wheel at her back, but he didn't care. Tammy needed reassurance, and by damn, he was going to give it to her.

Cramped or not, they managed to steam up the windows, fill the cab of his truck with the sweet aroma of her arousal, and give his springs a good rocking. He should have known he wouldn't get off that easy.

She waited until they got to his house before she gave him some payback.

When her cell phone rang, she dug it out of her pocket and answered. "Hey, Mom. Sorry I cut you off earlier. Things got kind of busy. Looks like

I'm going to be staying here a while." A stream of excited chatter came through the receiver. Tammy rolled her eyes. "No, they're not holding me prisoner. And, yes, this is my decision. I've met a guy, and we're going to try and make a go of it. You know, shack up together." More excited chatter and Reid shook his head. It sounded as if Tammy was getting an earful.

"Is he what?" Tammy's voice rose. "No, I am not asking him that. Tell you what, ask him yourself."

With a smirk, Tammy tossed him the phone and walked away, stripping as she went.

As Reid gaped at her bare backside as it swished up the stairs, it took him a moment to grasp what the female voice on the phone was asking. When he did, he could only repeat, "Did you just seriously ask me if the Northern Lights mutated my sperm?"

And what did his city girl do as he stammered his way through the most awkward conversation of his life? Laughed, winked, and disappeared upstairs.

When he finally managed to reassure Tammy's mother that no, he wasn't a psycho bearded woodsman who would keep her daughter locked in a shack to breed mutant Northern Light babies—although he was tempted at one point to mention they might have cubs—he tore up the stairs after his newly acquired mate.

He found her sprawled across his bed, reading. She rolled onto her back and smiled at him. "And now we're almost even."

"Almost? If you ask me, you owe me. I thought the frying pan and silver in the ass were bad, but conversing with your mom? Way beyond cruel."

She laughed. "You totally deserved it for keeping the whole I'm-now-a-bear thing secret."

"Speaking of secrets, your mom is coming for a visit."

"What?" Tammy sat up. "What for?"

"Why, to help plan the wedding of course." Did he sport an evil smile at the look of horror on her face? Yeah. He did.

"Wedding? What wedding?"

"Our wedding. It's not necessary because, technically, by shifter law, we're mated."

"Mated!" She yelled the word. "When did that happen?"

"When I announced it to the clan this morning at our meeting."

"Without asking me first?"

"I'm alpha. We don't ask. We declare."

"You're really pushing it, Reid."

"Not yet, but I will be." Right into her velvety softness.

"I'm really beginning to rethink this whole living together thing," she grumbled. "You're bossy."

"I thought we'd already ascertained you weren't leaving. Ever."

"Says you."

"Yes, says me."

"What I'd like to know is how we went from shacking up to getting married because I know for a fact we never discussed it."

"Minor details. Besides, I know how girls love that kind of thing. And your mom seemed real keen on it."

"I can't marry you. I'm not even sure I like you right now."

He pinned her to the bed and pulled her arms above her head. "Screw like. Admit it, you love my ass."

"It's big and hairy."

"So is yours now," he replied, only to wince as she kneed him uncomfortably close to a certain sensitive area. "I was talking about your polar one."

"Sure you were," she growled.

"Do I have to prove, once again, how much I love your rounded splendor? Please say yes."

Forget waiting for her answer. He showed her. Once. Twice. Stopped for some food. Then a third time.

As they lay in a curled heap, hours later, after he'd gotten her to admit she might, just might, love him a little, he smiled. Much like the gold miners had decades ago, this Kodiak had made his claim.

And if anyone dared harm the woman he loved with every fiber of his bearish being, he'd kill them, old friend or not.

Epilogue

A few weeks later, during the full moon.

The itching and irritability started a few days before the lunar event. Tammy equated it to a severe form of PMS, but to his credit, Reid bore it. He took all of her temper and foibles in stride. But before you thought he just caved to her and let her get away with it, it should be noted that Reid wasn't about to let anyone, not even his mate, walk all over him.

She yelled. He roared. She hollered again. He threatened to spank her. She dared him to try. He did. So she bit him. And they had wild sex.

Could she point out that she'd never been happier? Even when he finally got her to admit she loved him. He, of course, cheated though. After a particularly vigorous night, he brought her breakfast in bed, with, of all things, donuts brought in from the latest supply run.

Around a mouthful of sweet, melting goodness, she mumbled, "I wuv you."

To which he replied, "I love you, too."

With that first declaration out of the way, it became easy for Tammy to ease into her new life. As promised, Jan found her some work within the company, and they became the best of friends, which meant Tammy got an earful about that idiot, Boris. The same Boris that she heard got caught kissing Jan more than once, leaving her looking flustered, but pleased.

The upped patrols and vigilance that Reid instituted proved unnecessary. The attacks on the town and their vehicles stopped. Of Gene and his band of animal friends, not a sight or sound or hair was found. But Tammy knew Reid didn't trust this lull, and so the stepped-up protection remained.

Tammy wasn't afraid though. Despite her initial shock at her new state of being, she'd quickly adjusted to and learned it wasn't all bad. For one thing, she healed pretty damned quick now and felt great. The occasional animal roar and sprouts of hair and claws when she got emotional did kind of freak her out. As did the first time her bear tried to communicate with her in her mind. But where Reid sometimes failed to quell her panic, Ursula always came through.

Who knew chocolate chip cookie dough was the cure-all for just about any ailment? When that failed, upside-down, brown sugar-rich pineapple cake, still hot, with a scoop of vanilla ice cream, sure helped.

Life took on a pleasant routine. A happy one, marred by only one thing. Tammy's fear of her first change. Reid did his best to reassure her. "It's not that bad. You'll see."

As the full moon approached, while filled with trepidation, Tammy couldn't deny a certain element of excitement.

The first time she shifted, it took her breath away, not just because of the pain but because of the stream of curses she let out during the process, curses that turned into grunts and howls.

Bears don't howl. This one did. She did. *Ohmyfuckinggodlamabear.*

Even though her visual perspective was skewed, she had no trouble recognizing her hands were now paws and her ass was definitely a mile wide and covered in white fur.

She bellowed in shock, and Reid, whom she recognized now no matter what shape he wore, snorted. It gave her no small pleasure to cuff him in the side of the head and see him stagger. He might be a Kodiak, but she was a fucking polar bear. Hear her roar.

And see her run. But she preferred not to recall what she did in the woods with Reid. Surely there were laws against that.

When they eventually returned to the house, the change back to her human shape was just as bad as expected.

"Ow. Ow. Ow."

"Stop being such a pussy cat," Reid teased as he bundled her shivering frame into a blanket.

Teeth chattering from the cold, Tammy glared at him. "I will complain if I want to. That freaking hurt!"

"You'll get over it. And it will get easier."

"Over it? I'm never doing it again."

He dismissed her assertion. "Bah. The exhilaration of being your animal will make you forget, and you'll shift again, sooner than you think.'"

"Never. Too painful."

"So is childbirth, and yet women haven't stopped getting pregnant."

She waved a hand. "I'm planning on an epidural for that."

Reid laughed as he said, "I love you, city girl."

And she loved him. More and more each day.

*

There was a peculiar perversity in spying on people. In planning their demise. In devising ways to squash their irritating happiness.

There was also a depressing loneliness to living on the outskirts. Of being an observer to a world he once belonged to. A world that had shunned him and left him to die.

Gene knew those living in Kodiak point, especially his old platoon mates, watched for him. He'd seen the patrols and evaded them with ease. He'd not earned the nickname Ghost for nothing. Like a wisp of wind, a shadow barely seen, he slipped in and out of places with none the wiser.

Could he have killed the happy couple? Cocking an imaginary gun and eying down its barrel, he grinned. In a heartbeat.

But that was too easy. Too simple. Let them think they'd scared him off. Let them ease back into their happy little lives. It would make the shock of his next move all the sweeter.

Because this was not the end.

Next book in the series featuring a certain ornery moose and a wily vixen, Outfoxed by Love.

Printed in Great Britain
by Amazon.co.uk, Ltd.,
Marston Gate.